Books by HONOR TRACY

The Deserters
Kakemono: A Sketchbook of Postwar Japan
Mind You, I've Said Nothing!
The Straight and Narrow Path
Silk Hats and No Breakfast
The Prospects Are Pleasing
A Number of Things
A Season of Mists
The First Day of Friday

The First Day of Friday

Random House

New York

❀

The

FIRST
DAY
OF
FRIDAY

❀

a novel by

HONOR TRACY

❀

To Reggie Ross Williamson

The First Day of Friday

One

MICHAEL DUFF lay in his creaking four-poster bed and harkened drowsily to the rain as it drove with vehemence against the windows. His room was a vortex of draughts this April morning. There was the familiar gust that moaned down the chimney, bringing flurries of soot with it, and the one that whistled under the door, causing the threadbare old carpet to balloon excitedly, and the one that made its way in almost furtively through a cracked panel in the door that led to his dressing room. His experienced sense detected a newcomer in the throng today as well, one that he could not place or account for. Supine, with half-closed eyes, he thought about the patch of black fungus on the wall, a fungus that repelled him and fascinated him at the same time, like everything about his house, possessions and native land. The patch grew stealthily with every fall of rain and at present was roughly the size and form of a small, heavily laden ass, a Connemara ass, perhaps, carrying creels of turf. One day it would spread all over the wall's surface.

With a grinding noise the door of his bedroom opened and a female head came cautiously into view. Under a tangle of bright red curls was a wide peasant face from which peered out, in mingled cunning and dread, a pair of yellow cat-like eyes. "Master Michael, honey," a whining voice began.

Without a word Michael reached down for a slipper and hurled it with all his might in the direction of the head. This vanished at once, and Michael flung a second slipper at where it had been, an empty ritual act but one which brought him a kind of comfort. The woman could be heard shuffling away down the corridor and talking to herself in the same whining tone. Michael suddenly remembered a dream of the night before, in which the fungus and this creature had both figured. A tall queenly woman in flowing robes and bejewelled crown, like Caitlín ní Houlihán in a St Patrick's Day procession, had appeared and revealed to him that the black patch in truth was the map of Ireland. On that day, not perhaps far distant, when it should entirely cover the wall, Ireland would recover her Six Counties and Atracta Smith be proclaimed queen over all . . . Michael had cried out and jerked himself to a sitting position in his sleep. His last thoughts before dozing off had in fact been, as they often were, of Atracta, of something she had done, something so fantastically mindless as to make a normal brain spin to think of yet that was absolutely and completely like her to do. After every mealtime she was supposed to bring Michael's mother a glass of water and a pill, but it seldom occurred to her to do so. Mrs Duff made no objection, for she thought these pills terribly expensive: she would often declare that every time she took one she was swallowing sixpence. Yesterday Atracta had appeared after luncheon for once with the glass of water, but with a sixpence instead of the pill. She had placed the sixpence carefully on a clean saucer, and even went so far as to ask if an English sixpence would do since no Irish one could be found. Michael had driven her from the room in a passion. He had shouted that she ought to be flogged, tied up and severely flogged. He simply could not believe that anyone could do such a thing, that it was not some colossal impertinence on the woman's part. Mrs Duff told him that he was wrong: she explained that Atracta's mind was wholly taken up with dreams, which left her with no power of concentration and very little feeling for the life around her.

"What sort of dreams?" Michael had demanded.

"That, very likely, we shall never know," Mrs Duff replied after a pause.

Miles away in the village the bell of the parish church began to ring for eight o'clock Mass. At ten he had to be in Ballinaduff, to appeal against the new assessment of rates on Georgetown. At this time of the year with the roads flooded he could not be sure of getting to town in under an hour. Breakfast was ordered for eight o'clock sharp every morning, but it would be well past nine before Atracta had it on the table. He swung his legs over the edge of the bed and sat awhile, meditatively rubbing his head. The new draught played vivaciously over his neck and shoulders and, turning, he saw that one of the windows had slid a few inches down, in a lopsided way that defied any attempt to push it up. Best leave it as it was: best leave everything as it was. He went into the dressing room and poured some cold water from the cracked jug into the cracked bowl, wondering as he washed what had brought Atracta cringing to his door. She was forbidden ever to approach his room while he was inside: he had told her plainly that if she did he would not be responsible for what might happen. Last night he had informed her that breakfast would simply have to be punctual this morning, that there were no two ways about it, he had often said it before, he knew, but this time he absolutely meant it. She had sworn passionately to die before she let him down. Could it be, was it conceivable, that breakfast in fact was ready and she had come to announce it? No. But what else? Perhaps she had found out what his errand in Ballinaduff was to be, had learned by the local grapevine of the staggering new assessment on his house and buildings and had tumbled to the fact that if he could not get it cut this might well be the end for them all, that the last straw might be added and the back finally broken. He was half inclined to think this must be the solution. Atracta must have made the supreme effort of her career and got breakfast on the table before she was even asked to, from no loyalty to her young master but because she scented a danger to herself and her brood.

Hurriedly he shaved and dressed and went downstairs. On entering the dining room he found nothing ready at all. The room itself was in darkness and when he furiously pulled the curtains back he saw that yesterday's supper had not been cleared away. The plums and custard stood on the table, and on the sideboard were the beetroot-and-potato salad and the cold rabbit pie. Swearing, he made for the kitchen. Heavy swing doors shut the domestic quarters off from the rest of the house, and in the ordinary way the moment these were pushed open the shrieks and sobs of Atracta's triplets made themselves heard. Now there was dead silence except for the slamming of the outer kitchen door, which signified that it stood open to the yard to allow free passage to the prevailing wind. The kitchen was deserted, the boiler and the stove unlit, and a ginger cat was lapping milk from a can beside the door.

She is insane, Michael thought. Calm took possession of his soul, the benign, almost rueful calm that murderers are said to feel immediately before committing the act. He retraced his steps to the dining room, where, in a battered tartan dressing gown, his mother was helping herself to the rabbit pie.

"Atracta must go, Mother," he said gently.

"Yes, darling, of course." They often talked like

this together. "Certainly we are having rabbit pie rather often. And it is not a breakfast dish."

"I told her," he said piteously. "I told her, last night, last thing, that breakfast would have to be ready today. She said, 'May God strike me dead, Master Michael, if I should fail you.' "

"Those people drag the Almighty into everything," Mrs Duff observed. "Plums and custard too, I see. It seems only yesterday that we had them."

"Is she wicked, Mother? Or merely an imbecile?" It was the perennial question.

"I rather think that it must be religion," Mrs Duff said. "I imagine Atracta has gone to her chapel. They invariably do so when they are needed."

"In the middle of the week? The season isn't open yet. All those Assumptions and things are in the summer."

"Oh well, then, darling, it'll be because there's an R in the month or something of that kind," Mrs Duff said, carrying her plate of pie to the table and sitting down. "No knives or forks. Depend on it, the chapel is where Atracta has gone."

"And why the devil didn't she say so, last night?"

"She didn't know. Those people never think of anything until it is actually upon them. Give me a knife and fork, like a dear boy. I suppose we are not to have any tea."

"She shall go," Michael said, passing the implements to his mother. "She shall go without delay."

If he left at once he might be able to snatch a crust

and a cup of tea in Ballinaduff. He hurried outside for a word with the men and found that his mother must have been right. There was not a whistle to be heard, nowhere the smell of a cigarette. Ravenous turkeys, geese, hens and guinea fowl flew at him uttering indignant cries the moment he set foot in the haggard, cows lowed plaintively in their sheds and pigs revelled delightedly in the filth of the day before. Dano the stallion had broken his fence and in company with two little asses browsed in the ruins of a herbaceous border. Milk cans that by now should have been well on their way to the creamery lay drunkenly on their sides in the yard.

On the back seat of his ancient Ford lay Dilly the cat, with yet another trio of kittens. As he opened the door she looked up at him with yellow eyes that were lazy, impudent and watchful all at once. Her offspring, like Atracta's, were the spitting image of herself: there might never have been a father in either case. All that to-do, Michael thought, to produce three male replicas of Atracta Smith! He was back on the dreadful subject again. With a pang he remembered the explosion of joy some years ago when Atracta, holiday-making with an aunt in Bray, wrote to say she was engaged to a Mr Alfred Smith. The wedding had taken place, for abundant photographs were there to prove it. Yet only seven months later, while they still luxuriated in Atracta's absence, she had burst into the house, great, even enormous with child, and claimed protection, bread and re-employment, claimed them as a self-evident right on the

simple ground that her mother and grandmother had
served the family in the same indescribable fashion as she
herself had done. They had of course taken her in. What
the cause of the rift might have been they never learned,
for on this point the voluble Atracta was tight as a clam.
Despite the existence of Benedict, Patrick and Kevin,
Mr Alfred Smith remained a mysterious and shadowy
figure, almost a myth; but Atracta had burrowed, tick-
like, deeper into their lives than before.

Michael moved Dilly and her brood onto a bale of
straw and drove off. The rain had stopped and the morning was sharp, bright and tremulous, and a rainbow
swung over the sky. Michael slowed down a little once
he was out of the Georgetown trees to enjoy the sweep
of the countryside with the gorse in flower and scented
by the sun, and now and then a glimpse of faraway
blue sea. Then he glanced at his watch and trod on the
accelerator at once. What happened to time in this
demon-haunted land? It was twenty minutes to ten.
There was no question of having any breakfast, he would
not even be in time for the appointment. And if this
fellow were annoyed with him his appeal might not
succeed, and if his appeal did not succeed, why then, he
did not see how he could carry on.

They were trying to recoup themselves for the loss
of the Ballysimon rates. When the nuns acquired the
Court there had been the usual popular rejoicings. One
more alien stronghold had passed into the keeping of
Holy Church and the power of honest Gaels. One more

old Georgian building would be decently smothered in the grey ecclesiastical plaster that mottled all Ireland like a skin disease. But the nuns had lost no time in pointing out that the uses to which the convent would be put were such as to excuse them from paying any rates at all; and hence the amount had to be shared out among the few families who still clung on.

It had not, of course, been put that way. There had been the usual song about rising costs and improved services, but this was the truth, and in the unlikely event of his appeal being granted the extra burden would fall on others. So that there was a kind of hopelessness about the whole affair, and in him a kind of acquiescence, even the desire, for a state of things to arise in which no one could blame him for clearing off. He saw himself earning good English or Canadian wages, putting money by together with the proceeds of the George-town sale until Dulcie and he could set up in whatever they liked, a farm, orchards, a riding school. He did not in the least want to occupy the place in things which to his mother seemed a condition of remaining alive at all. He did not want to be the one who, in exchange for a little pointless deference, eternally decided, com-manded, paid, suffered, bore the brunt and hung on. But while he might cheerfully dispense with the former privileges of his state, he was still the captive of its modes of behavior. Things had to be done properly, he could not bear to rat.

He reached the county offices half an hour after the

appointed time, and the man he had come to see was not yet in. He sat on a bench in the hall, fuming at the unpunctuality of the Irish. Countrymen were coming and going with wooden faces, intent on the ramified little schemes so dear to their devious minds. Watching them Michael felt, as all through his life he had done, as if he lived in a foreign land. At ten minutes to eleven he was on the point of going away when Mr Collins dashed in and bore him off to his office.

"Oh, God, Mr Duff, what'll you think of me at all?" His manner was nervous and ingratiating. "Didn't it go clean from me head when we made the appointment that today was a first Friday?"

"A first . . . ?"

"A first Friday. The nine Fridays, you know. Salvation. St Margaret Mary Alacoque," Mr Collins explained, taking off his hat, coat and muffler and hurling them aside as if he never wished to see them again. He stuffed a jujube into his mouth and sat down at his desk, waving Michael to a chair.

St Margaret Mary à la Coque: the nine Fridays: salvation: how exotic it all did sound! Perhaps his mother could throw some light on it. "I got the assessment, Mr Collins. It's impossible. Can't be done. I'm up to my neck. I'd be a lot better off in a Lancashire mill."

"God help us, Mr Duff, wouldn't we all be that?" Mr Collins beamed upon the supplicant while his steady little eyes flitted over his face. "Why do we ever stick it out at all?" he asked, as man to man.

"You know how things are at my place," Michael proceeded. "I'll have to sell out, and that's all about it."

"Don't be talking, Mr Duff! You're the kind the country needs. The old families! The old stock!" cried Mr Collins, all but choking on the jujube at the very idea.

"I haven't paid the rates for the last year yet," Michael told him. "Perhaps I never shall."

"That's another department altogether," said Mr Collins primly.

"I'll turn the key in the door and steal away," Michael threatened.

"You wouldn't? Ah, you wouldn't?" Mr Collins besought him, clasping his hands together; for the county council had a humane dislike of killing off geese before the last golden egg was laid.

"I'll give the place to someone. What do I get from it? I bust myself keeping afloat, like a fellow swimming against the millrace. I'll give Georgetown to St Margaret Mary What's-it, for her Fridays. She won't be paying rates at all, if I know her." He leaned back in his chair and folded his arms, while his heart filled again with the gentle murderer's feeling.

"Mr Duff likes a joke." But was Mr Duff really joking? Mr Collins earnestly studied the young face with the heavy dark brows and square chin and the light that danced in the grey eyes. What did that light portend? Mr Duff did not at all seem like a man in despair or even seriously vexed. Old Major Buchanan had come in a few days ago on a similar errand and had been on the point of tears. Suppose Duff did sell out to some religious order? Mr Collins sucked his jujube and rubbed his scaly chin while his mind went ticking on. "I'll tell you what, now," he said at length, "I'll consult with me superior."

Mr Duff knew that as far as the Georgetown assessment was concerned, no such person existed. "You will?" he asked gravely.

"I'll do it this very day."

"Yes, you'd better." Michael got up, signifying that the interview was over, and without intending to Mr Collins helplessly stood up too. "Otherwise it will be St What's-it à la Coque for Georgetown. Remember!" He left the county buildings, chuckling as he went, and drove home dwelling voluptuously in his imagination on the scene to come.

Two

Mrs Duff, still in her dressing gown, was wandering up and down the hall like a frightened little ghost. "This came with the letters," she said, waving a piece of buff-coloured paper. "It looks official, but it is all in Molly." By this she meant that it was in the Gaelic tongue.

"Then it must be something of importance to you," Michael said. "When it is important to them, they write in English."

"What shall we do? How can we find out what it means?" she asked tremulously. Anything to do with the government reminded her of a little knot of short-legged men in dirty waterproof coats that she had seen one day.

"Don't worry, Mother. I'll see to it. Is Atracta here?"

"Yes, she came in just now."

"At half-past twelve!"

The familiar uproar greeted his ears as he pushed the swing doors back and was much intensified as he entered the kitchen. The red-headed yellow-eyed triplets were breaking their fast. Benedict and Patrick gobbled slices of bread and jam and gaily beat on the table with wooden spoons, while Kevin bawled out of some private sorrow, his cavernous mouth full of half-chewed bread. Atracta watched over them fondly, with a glass of stout in her hand and a line of froth on her upper lip.

"Atracta Smith! Where were you till this?" her master began, in passionless tones of doom.

She turned her cat's eyes on him indulgently, thinking the gentry were terrible ignorant. "Master Michael dear! Wasn't it the first day of Friday? And mustn't the little ones go to Mass? And didn't I come to you and tell you so, and you wouldn't hear me out?"

"And what did you do after that? Shut up, you brats."

It was the first time in their lives that he had ever addressed the children directly. Patrick and Benedict laid down their spoons in astonishment and Kevin howled more dreadfully than before.

"Sure, nothing at all, Master Michael. We ran straight here and never looked at the road behind us, the way you'd get your breakfast before you went to the town. And you were just gone out when we got here."

"You were blethering at the chapel door with the other women," Michael said. Each holy day of obligation was a morning lost. "The mistress told me the hour you got in."

"God love her, the poor lady!" Atracta exclaimed, eliminating Mrs Duff as a responsible witness. "But the Mass was terrible long today, oh, 'twas shocking. The priest was reading out a cyclamen from the new Pope. 'Twas all about surgery, Master Michael," she continued on a note of triumph, as if glorying in her powers of recollection, " 'twas how surgery was a mortal sin and diabolical, setting one man against the other and completing the ends of justice: and there's all too much of it in Ireland today: and from this day forth anyone committing surgery can't get confession from Father Behan but has to go to the Bishop himself, and be roasted . . ."

"Stop it!" her master screamed. Atracta's expositions of her faith unmanned him altogether. Controlling himself, he went on: "Now make that child be quiet. I have something to say."

The gentleness of his tone brought a look of apprehension into the broad face at last. Atracta snatched the scarf from her head and wound it tightly round Kevin's, round and round and round while the noise grew fainter and eventually died.

"What did I tell you about breakfast?" Michael began.

"Oh, God, Master Michael, love, I wouldn't have wished it . . ."

But why start a discussion, Michael thought, because this time the decision is irrevocable, really and truly final. He cut her short and said almost lovingly, "I am sorry, Atracta, but you will have to go."

He thought he knew what would follow, because he was sacking her now for the nineteenth time. There would be a wild outcry with the pent-up grief of centuries behind it, like the keening of professional mourners at the bier. After would come a torrent of passionate entreaty, in which the sufferings of a forsaken wife with three little innocent ones to feed and clothe would figure not at all. Atracta had but one reaction to any misfortune or humiliation that might publicly befall her: what would the township of Crummagh say? To be shamed before that community of four hundred souls, to her mind, was the ultimate disaster. Equally, nothing was of importance in itself but only as regards what others might think of it: thus she did not at all object to the thought of lying or stealing but only to that of being called a liar or a thief. She would cry out that it would be better for Master Michael to kill her stone dead itself than drive her from his doors with the name of a bad servant. As a rule he would counter her appeals with his own arguments, his voice growing louder and angrier as his determination weakened until at last he would shout that she had one more chance, and only one, before he stormed out of the kitchen. The very frightfulness of the woman in truth was her trump card: that bottomless primeval stupidity, shot by intermittent flashes of cunning, laid an obligation almost as inescapable as if she were bodily afflicted.

Atracta did not break into the customary ululation at all but simply bowed her head without a word, gazing sadly at the foam on her stout.

"At the end of the month, Atracta, please," he said, marvelling at her composure and apprehensive of it at the same time. "You may stay in your cottage until you are settled in another place."

"God bless you, honey love," she said in broken tones, as if he had made her a substantial and unhoped-for present.

"Bridie may come in and learn the ropes while you're still here," he continued, wondering what devilry she might be up to now.

A spark did appear in the yellow eyes at that and Atracta seemed to be on the verge of protesting. Then Kevin began to buzz like a bee under the scarf that bound his head, and while the fact of his peril slowly penetrated the clouds of her mind and she puzzled as to what steps could be taken Michael made his escape.

"I've done it!" he said joyfully to his mother, who was making her lunch of the cold rabbit pie and beetroot salad. The official paper was propped against the salad bowl before her and she watched it steadily as she ate, as if daring it to make a move. "She is to go at the end of the month."

"I am very pleased to hear it," Mrs Duff replied. "We have already had a rabbit pie this week, of that I am convinced. People of that class have so little imagination. Darling, can't you sit down a moment?" for

Michael was hacking himself a piece from the loaf to take away.

"I can't, everything is hopelessly behind," he said, buttering it. "And all through someone, something, à la coque. Let me have old Molly. Are you not going to dress at all today?"

Mrs Duff looked down and caught sight of her bedroom attire. "Good heavens!" she exclaimed. Michael was halfway to the door.

The image of himself he had given Mr Collins as a man swimming against a millrace was accurate, and when there was a weekday Mass it was as if the swimmer had paused for breath and in a minute been swept a hundred years back. It would take him all day now to struggle up to where he should have been in the morning. One of his chief troubles was that he had not a single man on whom to depend. Tomo was honest by local standards but he drank; Paddy was sober but given a chance would steal the clothes from your back; John neither drank nor stole but was so thick-witted that Michael often thought him worst of all. The same orders had to be given time and again, all must be explained and repeated and supervised, and on top of it all he had to contend with the peasant stubbornness, the iron determination under all the blarney to suit themselves and do whatever they felt inclined. Munching away at his bread and butter he thought of the day that, walking round the estate with the English cousin, he had come on Tomo blind drunk under a hedge that he was supposed to be cleaning, with his implements strewn about over the ground. He had retraced his steps without a word, filled two buckets from the well, returned to where the unconscious Tomo lay and dashed the contents of both over his head. Cousin Nathaniel was in ecstasies, regarding this procedure as something typically Irish and delightful. "You're so *human* in this country!" he cried. "In England the poor fellow would have been sacked." He drivelled on about humanity and spiritual values and life being meant for living until Michael could gladly have hit him. If he sacked Tomo he would get, if he got anyone at all, someone every bit as bad and perhaps not such agreeable company. The good men all cleared off to England and small blame to them: wasn't he longing to do the very same thing?

The very thought of sacking anyone, however, turned his mind to Atracta again and his heart grew light within him. The load that had been lifted from his back was one which, he now felt, he could not have endured for another day. Bridie Larkin should do the cleaning, he decided, and Mrs Beamish should be appointed cook: household matters fell to him along with all else, for Mrs Duff took refuge in total vagueness when called on to do anything whatsoever. How delightful the future would be! A zany little song sprang up in his head:

The first day of Friday the new Pope gave to me
A cyclamen and a little surger-ee.

Now why, he mused, should the new Pope have taken against surgery? Perhaps Atracta was mistaken in believing that he had. Or might it not be something to do with the resurrection of the body? Someone had told him once that the medical students in Dublin had an awful time of it, keeping the anatomy-school corpses each to itself. Then what about those poor dear missionaries, munched up by the natives? These were matters too deep for the finite human mind. He began singing aloud, "The first day of Friday . . ."

There was the sound of hooves on the gravel behind him and a gruff voice said, "Evening, Michael."

"Oh! Good evening, Master," he said, startled. "What brings you our way?"

"I left some lilac for your mother," the Master of Foxhounds said. "A great year for lilac. There was no one about, so I left it in the hall. And a note of the Hunt Ball for you. Late this year, but the Chairman is still in plaster. We didn't see much of you last season, Michael."

"Oh, Master, there's a terrible lot to see to here," he pleaded.

"Shut up, you brute," the Master said. She was addressing her mare. "All very fine, Michael. We mustn't let go."

"No, no," he murmured.

"Your father never missed a day. Or your grandfather." The Master had a clear recollection of most days out in her country over a period of sixty years. "People expect to see a Duff, y'know."

"Yes, Master," he said meekly.

"I came by the Crummagh road just now," the Master said, shortening her reins. "Your wall is down.

Going to be a bother getting it up. Goodbye." She trotted on.

Michael looked after the lean figure in the shabby coat and breeches and thought of all the crisp autumn days when he would have given a great deal to down tools and ride out with the others. Upon his soul, it was hard to be blown up for so bravely resisting the temptation! People expected to see a Duff, did they? He dared say they did. There was only one Duff and people apparently expected to see him in five different places at a time. He must get the car out and go look at the wall. Not a man had mentioned that it was down, although all of them would have passed it on the way to their chapel: just like them, the devils.

His heart sank when he saw the damage and tried to reckon up the cost of repair. This wall was a high, venerable one that ran all round the property and was made of boulders and stones piled one on the other with seeming nonchalance but in fact with a skill growing rare in these days. There was an ugly gap in it now, nearly two yards wide, due partly to age, partly to the heavy rains of the winter and partly to being used as a stile by the villagers when they came to collect firewood. Through the breach Michael could see the path they had worn for themselves through the thicket. There was timber in plenty at Georgetown and he had always allowed the people to take what they needed. The only condition he made was that they should come and go by one of the gates and refrain from damaging growth;

but in their mysterious way they preferred to sneak in like tinkers and tear the branches from the trees, as if the mock-robbery of the landlord and the harming of his property were old tribal rites that it was incumbent on them to carry out. Now the old wall was down and the stones lay about on the earth, one more little corner of ruin in crumbling tumbling bloody old Ireland; and it would have to be botched up anyhow, with blocks, with cement, for there was no money to repair it decently, and everyone passing that way might see how Georgetown was going to the deuce.

"What did Molly say?" his mother demanded the instant she saw him again.

"Oh, Lord! I quite forgot her."

Apart from the priest, the Presentation nuns and the Christian Brothers, the only Irish-speaking adult in the locality was Mr Foley, the postmaster. It was widely believed that he owed his place to proficiency in this respect, as other qualifications had never been discerned. Wearily Michael got the car out again and drove the three-odd miles to Crummagh, thinking that the first day of Friday seemed to be going on forever. The post office had a pleasant homely feel about it, being a liquor bar and a general store as well. Butter, stamps, paraffin, boots, Miraculous Infants of Prague, whiskey, all snuggled down together and, at this particular moment, the outgoing mail of the day reposed on a corner of boiled ham till the van should arrive to collect it. Mr Foley's little eyes glistened under their bushy brows as young Mr Duff came in. There was a prehensile quality about him that was quite remarkable, and people who went in for a postal order or a quarter-pound of cheese stuck by the hour like flies in gum. He regarded himself as one of Crummagh's leading intellectuals, a little below the priest and the doctor, on a straight level with the chemist and much above the undertaker and the Sergeant of Guards. Since all of these, irrespective of ranking, fled when they saw him approach, he was a man starved of intelligent commerce. The very prospect of it caused him to quiver all over, like a terrier promised a run. He was particularly pleased to see who the visitor was, because his account with Georgetown had run on now for three and a half years and this gave him, he thought, a kind of lien on its master. From the way he beamed and sparkled and rubbed his hands he appeared all set to bog Mr Duff down till midnight at the least. Yet as the nature of Michael's errand was explained to him the rapture all died away and he looked both hurt and offended, gingerly taking the paper from him as if it might bite.

"I'm indeed sorry for bothering you," Michael said.

"Wait now, till I get me glasses," Mr Foley said gruffly. He took out his spectacles, breathed at them, rubbed them up and slowly put them on. He at once took them off again, rubbed them and put them back. Now he scrutinized the paper for a while, his lips moving silently like those of a man in prayer. He sighed heavily and he groaned; and at last, waving the paper, excitedly broke into fluent speech.

"The Irish language!" he declaimed. "The official

tongue of our native land and no one can speak it! Can it revive? Should it revive? Are we wasting the energies of some of the ablest in the land? Are we crippling the brains of our youth?"

Michael listened to this tirade with all the calm of despair. "Is it from a government department, I wonder?" he asked.

"To compose this has taken a man's time," Mr Foley pointed out. "Copies will have gone about the country, burdening the mails. Up and down, busy men like yourself will be looking, I suppose, for someone to tell them what's in it. Time, Mr. Duff, time, time, time! the one commodity in Ireland that is never in short supply."

"I'm afraid I'm taking up yours," Michael said. Reaching his hand out he said casually, "What's this, the date of it was?" If he could only get the paper back he might break and run for it if anyone else came into the shop. But Mr Foley whisked it away directly, as if after all he had taken rather a fancy to it.

"And there in Dublin our rulers sit," he proceeded with gloomy relish, "glorying in our mystification!"

The telephone began to ring, on a plaintive resentful note as if it were accustomed, but not resigned, to being ignored.

"That's Ballinaduff head office for you," Mr Foley commented with a weary shrug. "Telegrams! by day and by night. Birth, death, racing results. The dead hand of the Civil Service," he resumed with fresh spirit, "the mummified unproductive hand of what, for lack of a better term, I shall call the bureaucracy . . ."

A freckled little girl in the cotton overalls of the convent school came in with a basket and shopping list and Mr Foley pounced on her with a shout of triumph. "Now, Mary," he said, "you'll show Mr Duff your prowess as a scholar and your feeling as a daughter of Erin. Read over that in English to him, like the great girl. The younger generation!" he said in an aside to Michael. "Isn't everything done for them? Aren't they fed with a spoon? I was out at work when I was a chiseller the age of this one: and look at me now." Having stated the case against formal education in this conclusive manner, he complacently folded his arms. The telephone gave vent to a prolonged shriek of protest and he lifted the receiver like a man badgered past enduring. "I'll be with you in just a minyoot," he said, and hung up. "Now, Mary, please!"

The girl blushed hotly and, taking the paper, began in a frightened whisper: "A chara! O friend!"

"Mr Duff will know that much," Mr Foley reproved her. "It is the body of the communication, the gist of the message as it were, that he'll want to come at."

Mary appeared to be on the brink of tears. " 'Tis the way the husks of the cattle food are there, sir, and to be cleansed with fire, and the people's servants to be given the power by the . . . by the . . . the greyhound . . . no, the warrior . . . no, the noble lady virgin . . .

of Duff, sir . . ." Her voice faltered and faded away altogether.

"Why, Mary, that's capital," Michael said. It seemed to make better sense than anything he had heard all day. "You couldn't tell me who is writing all this, I suppose?"

Mary threw a despairing glance round her and mumbled, "The people's servants in Dublin. 'Tis how danger may come to the land by the husks of the cattle fodder."

"And we pay taxes!" Mr Foley exclaimed, throwing wide his arms. It was a favourite cry of his, to fall back on whenever he was at a loss.

Mary broke down and wept.

"Come, child," Michael said, deftly recovering the paper while Mr Foley's arms were still extended. "No need to cry—you're an ornament to Ballysimon!"

He tore out of the shop before Mr Foley could stop him, recklessly implanting in the orator's bosom a rancour that would last as long as life. All at once he could bear no more. It was a peculiarity of his native land that to endure the ordinary round of life there called for an extraordinary frame of mind. And he was famished. He drove up Crummagh main street singing to himself in a dry demented voice,

"The first day of Friday the new Pope gave to me,
A greyhound, a warrior, a virgin, a cyclamen and
a little surger-ee. . . ."

✿

Three

✿

Now Mrs Duff was gazing spellbound at the television, which was a new experience in her life and one which neither she nor her son had ever thought to enjoy. Luxuries were not for the likes of them. It was true that Michael's godfather Ballysimon had snapped up one of the first sets ever marketed in Ballinaduff, but Ballysimon had won a prize in the Sweep. Poor dear Ballysimon's true passion had been for fast motor cars, and on his eightieth birthday he had treated himself to a Mercedes sports model, a monster that looked and travelled like a jet-propelled aeroplane. After a short reign of terror he had been disqualified from driving for life and in despair, for he regarded himself as a still youngish man, he had turned to television. Ever since he had been glued to his set in mingled horror and delight. On great occasions friends and neighbours were invited to watch with him and Michael had come with his mother to see both the coronation of Her Majesty and the wedding of Princess Margaret. Transported, they had gazed at the magical thing, never dreaming for one moment that it could ever be theirs. Then all of a sudden the berry-scarlet face and snowy beard of Nathaniel Edward William St. George, Viscount Ballysimon, were seen no more about the winding lanes of the County Drumanagh. On his ninety-fourth birthday he sawed off the branch of an elm tree on which he was perching astride and brought his career to an untimely end. With him, an epoch seemed to pass. His heir, fishing pearls in Tasmania, refused to come home, Ballysimon Hall went up for sale and the contents were auctioned off. Nuns acquired the old house for a song and Michael got the television set for another: Tomo the handyman fixed it up with the stimulus and support of a gallon of stout; and there at last it was, installed in a corner of their great windswept drawing room.

"It is like a breath of fresh air," Mrs Duff said happily as Michael came in. They could just make out the shadowy figure of the Duke of Edinburgh opening a boot factory in the Midlands. But, "I am not sure if I should want to live in England," she said, when the Duke had finished speaking. "The climate over there appears to be worse than our own." What with the age of the set, the distance from England and Tomo's pioneering efforts at installation, visibility was marred by what looked like a heavy downpour. "At least, in Ireland, it does not rain indoors."

"That isn't rain, Mother," Michael replied. "It is interference."

"Really? How very odd. Why does the Duke put up with it?"

"Hush."

The scene changed now to one of tremendous animation in a faraway land. There were flashing smiles and waving arms, windows were shattered, flower wreaths rode gaily above frenzied babyish faces, there was a tumult of shouting and singing, motor cars were overturned and buses set on fire.

"Why are they all so angry?" Mrs Duff wished to know. She had been particularly intelligent once but nowadays everything had to be explained to her: the assassination of her husband had somehow drawn a line through her life, as if closing a ledger.

"They aren't angry. They have been given their independence and have proclaimed a republic."

Mrs Duff considered the matter. "I am quite sure dear Ballysimon would not have approved of that," she said. Plainly she felt that Ballysimon's television set might have paid closer attention to Ballysimon's wishes. "I imagine that is why their faces are all so dirty," she went on. "Cleanliness is invariably the first thing to go in republics."

"It isn't dirt, Mother. They are Africans."

"*Africans*, Michael?" Mrs Duff meditated again. "I am surprised that the Queen allows it," she observed.

"Do wake up, dear heart. The Queen sent a message to congratulate them all. The man with the feathers in his hat read it out."

"Did she really? And she looks such a sensible girl. It is a very great mistake," Mrs Duff asserted with warmth, "to encourage people of that sort. Turn it off, darling."

"Oh," she gasped, the moment the lights went on, "what did Molly say?"

He looked at her in sudden tender pity. "Mr Foley wasn't sure," he confessed. "I'll have to try somewhere in the morning."

"Oh, Michael."

"Did you see the lilac, Mother?" he asked, to change the subject. "The Master left in a bunch for you." But not a petal or leaf of lilac was anywhere to be found. Michael shouted for Atracta, who came wearing a look of pious forgiveness and denying that lilac had ever been left in the house; and this new mystery taken together with the hag-like obduracy of Molly reduced Mrs Duff to a pitiful state of terror.

"I'll run old Molly up to Father Behan," Michael told her soothingly. "He'll quench her in a minute. Have dinner, now, and I'll eat something when I get in."

As he drove yet again along the road to Crummagh he thought again of the new republic and of the wild, happy dancing people. The commentator had spoken of the wind of change and the phrase echoed in his brain, firing his imagination. He felt this wind as a real one, blowing over the face of the world, sweeping through the dusty corners of life: he saw people waking in the morning and springing up to do new things, things unlike those they had done the day before, he saw habits falling away, duties flung off like broken chains, people mapping out their paths in freedom . . . She is going: he thought; she is really going and her brats with her. Immediately after breakfast I put the house, the farm, the lands on the market. I sack the men. The beasts are auctioned off. The wind of change, the wind of change! Shall only Africans be free? Of all the fantasies darting about in his mind this wicked irresponsible one was second favourite. The first of course was that in which, married at last, he lived with Dulcie on unencumbered land, surrounded by children, horses and red setters. He loved to imagine himself turning the key in the front door and stealing away with all his possessions left behind, like any Connemara peasant. But never before had he linked this fantasy to events in the world outside; indeed, he had all but forgotten there was such a place. Every morning the *Irish Times* of the day before arrived by post and, once Mrs Duff had looked through the obituaries, was consigned to the kitchen unread. He relied on Paddy or Tomo for news and might look to Mr Foley for its interpretation. Now this crackling growling spluttering box and the murky little screen bespangled with blinding dots and dashes had brought the outer world before his very eyes and ears. It exhilarated him to know that somewhere his fellow men were demanding and obtaining the freedom for which he hungered. Somewhere there were human beings who, thanks to their own energy and resolution, could get up or stay in bed, hoe their yams or craze themselves with drink, go to prayer meeting or boil their mothers for lunch, as the fancy took them. Michael was often bored or annoyed by his mother but he loved her and he would not have dreamed of boiling her for lunch, or for any other meal. What he did so thoroughly approve was the principle whereby each man could decide for himself in the matter. It was that, yes, it was precisely that, he reflected, that was bitter in his own life, it was that cruel absence of any choice at all, it was the eternal must must must: not even ought, but must.

The parochial house loomed up before him, a large, horrible specimen of the Victorian gothic revival, whose present occupant was Father Behan. He was an immensely tall, stooping man with the melancholy face of a basset hound, who had come to Crummagh from a Liverpool mission two or three years ago and was said to be mad. Only one window in the house was lit, and that poorly, and as Michael walked up the path to the door he heard a loud passionate voice holding forth within.

"Blessed Teresa was right," it exclaimed. "Oh,

Blessed Teresa had the length of *your* foot! It's a wonder you have any friends at all."

The young man hesitated, unwilling to intrude upon what seemed to be a quarrel; but no more was heard and presently he rang the bell. The light vanished from the window and through the stained-glass panel in the door he saw it coming down the passage. Father Behan opened the door, candle in hand, and peered out into the darkness with such a melancholy countenance as Michael thought he had never seen.

"It's Duff of Georgetown, Father," he said. "But you've company, I suppose."

"Not at all, I'm alone," Father Behan replied. "Come in, Michael, you're welcome." He spoke as if he had known him for years, although they had never before exchanged a word. He led the way into his parlour and, setting the candle on the bare deal table, motioned his visitor to a chair. Two wooden chairs and this table, indeed, were all the furniture in the room and there was no fire in the grate. The priest appeared to be camping uncomfortably and gracelessly in a house far too big for him like the Duffs themselves, and in contrast to his predecessor who had been surrounded with every genteel cosiness known to man.

On hearing of Michael's difficulty Father Behan took the paper from him and held it up to the flickering light. "From the Customs in Dublin," he said. " 'A chara, a parcel from overseas has arrived in this office addressed to Virginia Duff, the contents of which are packed in straw. As no certificate of health accompanies the packing, it cannot be permitted to enter the country, under the regulations concerning Colorado Beetle and Foot and Mouth Disease. Kindly send, together with this note, authority for the packing to be burned forthwith, failing which the parcel and contents will be returned to sender. Sine le meas.' "

This man is not mad, Michael thought. "Well, thank you very much, Father! That's a weight off my mind." There was a quality in the priest so direct and simple that he thought he would risk a little joke. "Mind you, you owed me something for keeping my people all morning, reading them cyclamens from the new Pope!"

The effect of these words was remarkable. Father Behan gave a violent start and, turning his long heavy face to Michael with a look of anguish on it, shuddered from head to foot and closed his eyes. Then in a low urgent tone he said: "We have no new Pope. And the Holy Father has sent no encyclical. And I never keep them over the half-hour on a working day." He clasped his great hands together and bowed his grey head over them for a while; and then mastering himself with an effort, he looked up again and went on: "Last Sunday I read them a pastoral from the new Bishop. I daresay they were referring to that." Another spasm racked the long ungainly figure.

Michael had no wish to pry into matters as delicate as these appeared to be, but there was one question he felt he must ask. "Was it about surgery?" he inquired in a hushed voice.

"No no no," cried Father Behan, with bitter patience. "Perjury. It was an admonition on the evils of perjury, and a direction that henceforward in this diocese it would be a reserved sin." He rose abruptly to his feet. "Thank you for coming, child," he said. Taking the candle he got up and walked ahead to the door, which he opened without a word, plainly dismissing the caller, and yet in such a way that Michael could not possibly object to it.

The young man drove home feeling both amused and touched. Father Behan's flock would have it that he was wrong in the head and yet, in under two minutes, how much had he not cleared up! He was conscious of feeling a curious bond with him, as if together they shared some secret and between them carried some load. Next his thoughts turned to the new Bishop and his pastoral of the Sunday before, and he recollected hearing rumours of disturbance in His Lordship's intellect as well. Hardly was he installed in the diocese, for one thing, than he openly declared that religion was a matter of faith, hope and love, and not of Mass-going or bead-telling! And other wild talk along those lines. Now came this new declaration, which would strike at the very roots of Irish justice if heeded, besides bringing the legal business of the land to a full stop. It was no wonder at all if the local tongues were a-wag.

Meanwhile at Georgetown Mrs Duff had forgotten

both lilac and Molly. She had begun her dinner and then, suddenly bethinking her of the television again, had left everything and run to it. She had pushed, pulled, twisted and prodded the knobs of the set until at last the grotesque figures reappeared among the dazzling showers of rain and the scarcely human voices began to bawl and rumble. As her son came into the room she held up one tiny thin hand and said, "Please be quiet."

Her habit of sending him off on urgent affairs and promptly forgetting all about them would rouse him to fury as a rule, but now the sweet prospect of dining excluded all other ideas. There was one thing to be said for Atracta's regime, namely, that one could eat at any hour of the night since all was left undisturbed on the table until it was time for breakfast. Indeed it was true in a general way, he reflected, that the so aggravating weaknesses of the Irish character had a comfortable side to them. Smiling, he opened the dining-room door and switched on the light, to discover the table cleared and polished and not a vestige of food anywhere.

The reason for this extraordinary and unprecedented state of affairs lay in Atracta's interpretation of her young master's conduct earlier in the day. Her way and Michael's of judging the same set of circumstances lay so far apart that no rapprochement ever was likely. To begin with, her mind received with difficulty the idea that he, or anyone, could be genuinely dissatisfied with her. To herself she was such a paragon that his rages, cursings and hurlings of small light objects at her person merely reflected an inner stress of his own, unrelated to anything she might have done. His dismissal of her, every so often, fell into the same category; but in the present case there was an entirely new feature and one that had set her thinking hard.

Coming into the hall she had found on the stand there a great armful of twigs with tender leaves and sweet blue flowers; and at once drew the inference that they were a gift or, as she phrased it to herself, a floral tribune from Master Michael. There was, that she could perceive, no other explanation possible. Master Michael had been too proud to come begging her pardon and telling how much he valued her work, and indeed she wouldn't have wished it, the Family was the Family, and she liked this delicate shamefaced way of making amends. When Master Michael began storming in his usual tone about the lilac, which she assumed was something to eat, she put it down to natural embarrassment. To show that she understood and forgave she had been working harder than ever and putting all kinds of thoughtful little touches here and there: not only clearing the table but wiping the fungus from the master's bedroom wall and giving his best new riding-boots a wonderful clean and rub.

Now she sat before the fire in the kitchen, happy and fulfilled, with the triplets round her. She had made supper for them and crammed it into their mouths, had fashioned from one of Mrs Duff's linen pillow slips a loin cloth for Benedict, who had taken to wetting his bed, and now she was giving them out the rosary. "Hay Mary fuller gray sir Loris widdye . . ." she intoned, her yellow cat's eyes devoutly shut: and the three young voices, hard as blades, bounced back: "Ho Mary mith'rav Go pray fruss inners now . . ."

Michael waited grimly outside the door until the mechanical chanting should end. It seemed at one moment likely to go on forever; but at last he heard Atracta, in a different, horrible and unctuous voice, commanding: "And now say a prayer for Master Michael."

"We will not!" the trio riposted as one.

"Our Lord forgave his murderers," Atracta reproved them, in the same repulsive voice as before.

"Go 'way!" they chorused.

The young master knocked on the door and went in. He had resolved to state his requirements in a dignified, not unkindly manner and the fewest possible words and to leave at once. The first thing his eye fell on was the missing lilac stuffed into an old paint pot and adorning the kitchen dresser. "Atracta, you bloody old fool!" he shouted. He thrust his hands into his pockets, as if uncertain of what they might not do if left at large. Then with a huge effort he continued softly: "I thought you didn't see the lilac that was left in for the mistress."

"Is it that old stuff, sir?" Atracta quavered. She sensed that somewhere or other down the line her reasoning had been at fault. "Ah, Master Michael, love, I wouldn't have wished it . . ."

"Get me bread, cheese and a bottle of stout," he ordered, his mind awhirl with passion.

"The stout . . . the stout . . . the stout does all be elucidated, Master Michael . . ." All language to Atracta served as a smoke screen, and the longer the word the denser the protection.

"Get me the bread and cheese, then. Hurry." Two dozen of stout, he knew, had been delivered the Tuesday before.

When she brought his meal he swallowed it down in great bites, glaring at her and her brood as he did so. They cowered together in fear, thinking it a desperate stroke that bound their lives to his. He slammed the empty plate on the table without a word and strode up the stairs three at a time to bed. He could hear the television squawking away like mad in the drawing room. On his wall was the huge grimy smear where the patch of fungus had lived and flourished; and in the middle of the carpet under the light there stood and shone, where he could not fail to see them, his fine tan riding boots, cleaned lovingly and irremediably with black polish.

The first day of Friday had drawn to its close; and the wind of change had apparently dropped.

※

Four

※

ALL during that night a gale from the Atlantic howled
and shrieked, shrieked and howled on a note of despair
and entreaty as if imploring someone to let it out of
somewhere. Now and again it died away to a subdued
heart-rending sob and the distant sea could be heard thud-
ding angrily on the shore. Presently it would get up, and
shriek anew, more frantic than ever, unable to think that
its supplication should go unheeded. The limes in the avenue and the house itself were yawning and sighing like
old old creatures who wonder if the end will never
come.

Michael listened to the racket with exasperation as
he lay in bed. It was a storm to bring trees down by
the dozen and slates off the roofs in avalanches. Another
such gale had blown only a few weeks before and, gam-

bling on its being the last of the winter, he had had everything put in order, as he hoped, until autumn. Now all was to do again. When morning came the wind was still at full strength and at breakfast time he merely gulped down a cup of tea and made for the door.

"Where are you going?" his mother asked at once.

"I'll have to run round the place and see what the damage is," he told her with a glance at his watch. They were notably late this morning, as Atracta had expended her reserves of energy the evening before.

"But you never told me about Molly," she complained. He had, of course, but she had not been able to take it in. She principally wished to know what the parcel contained and where it came from, and she could not fix her mind at all on the straw. There was, too, something strange in them asking for the note itself to be returned: at that rate why, she puzzled, send it out in the first place? "Depend upon it," she had remarked, with a wise little nod, "they are up to no good." She would have liked very much to discuss the programme of the evening before as well. There had been an interview with a dockyard matey, a dreadfully common little man, and questions had been put to him about his job, his life, his girl friend, the hostel he lived in, whether he drank or smoked or went to church and what he thought of Space. He answered them all, and finally asked if he might make a statement. His Christian name was Len, he revealed: his best friend's name was Len, his brother-in-law's name was Len and his fiancée's name was Lena! *And* all four of them had birthdays within a week! Coincidence? He rather thought so. He left the studio overcome with laughter, amid tumultuous applause.

Mrs Duff had thought the whole affair a mistake and in very poor taste. Ballysimon would have had no patience with it. She did not choose to know the Christian names of people of that sort, and as for birthdays, they were better without them. For that matter, it was a pity to notice the lower classes at all, as they got excited and above themselves as children did. She would have liked to go thoroughly into the question with Michael, and there he was racing off as usual. She might as well, she often said, have had no son at all.

"Did you hear that? Wasn't it a car engine?" he asked, stopping short. "You can hear nothing with this wind. It sounded like our own." He hurried to the window in time to see the motor disappearing through the wind-tossed trees of the avenue. "Good heavens above!" He tore out to the haggard and shouted for the men, who came slowly forward looking sheepish and unhappy.

"He'd no right to do that, sir, no right at all," Tomo said, avoiding Michael's eye.

"He's not entitled," Paddy said, staring at the ground. "You could sue him, I'd say."

"But who was it? What does he want? I need the car, I'll have to be driving round till I see what's up and what's down."

"He did say, sir, that he was from the rate collector's office, in a manner of speaking," Tomo replied, delicately looking away.

A kind of horror came over the master of Georgetown then, a sudden chilling intimation of the underlying ruthlessness of the native character. Ireland had all the cosy warmth of the reptile house in a zoo, he thought: you were lapped in blarney and butter until the moment your means of livelihood were seized or your father was shot. He rushed back into the hall and flung himself at the telephone, startling his mother as she advanced on the family portraits with a feather duster in her hand.

"They drove off the car," he said breathlessly.

"Michael! but how shall we get to church?"

"Church, Mother!" He broke into a merry young laugh and felt a little better. "Church is tomorrow."

He stood with the receiver to his ear, wondering as time passed if the lines were down in the storm. In his distraction he had forgotten that the old system had recently been swept away and a dialling code brought in, in harmony with modern practice the world over. The days were gone when you exchanged a pleasant word or two with the operator before you asked for a number: to be told, perhaps, that himself was not there at all this morning, he went to the town, wait now till I corner him for you. As the minutes ticked by, however, the truth sank in. Furiously he seized the telephone book to find out where, numerically speaking, he was and how to come at the rate collector, turning page after page in dismay, for he was a man of action and of the open air with no taste or mind for paper work at all. At last he had it worked out, he carefully dialled, gratefully listened to the ring of the bell and then, with a sense of nightmare, heard the voice of Mr Foley.

"There's a fault in the system, I'm afraid," Michael said. "I'm trying for the county offices."

Mr Foley's manner cooled when he realized who was speaking but any audience was better than none. "Science! Technique! Progress!" he began. "But has the moral development of Man kept pace . . ."

Michael audaciously pressed down the bar, hoping Mr Foley would ascribe the sudden rupture to a fresh caprice of the mechanism. After waiting a minute or so, he lifted it again and prepared to start anew.

". . . a roof, a plot of land, me own cow, me own potatoes," Mr Foley was rumbling on.

How in the name of God had he worked himself round to that? Michael wondered. "Mr Foley, I'm very sorry, but it's an emergency," he said. "I'm in trouble all right. You couldn't get me through to the county offices, I suppose? In the old-fashioned way?"

"I could not," Mr Foley freely admitted. He sounded more grieved than offended now. "I may as well be honest with you, Mr Duff. I don't understand the bloody thing at all. And I'm the postmaster!" he added, in sombre triumph. "Would you care at all to give me an inkling of the nature of your dilemma?" It sounded as if he thought this might have a bearing on the telephonic communications of the area.

Nosy bastard, Michael thought; but he would never struggle out of the web till Mr Foley's desires were assuaged. "It looks as if my car was stolen," he said.

"The Lord save us!" the postmaster ejaculated. "That's crime."

"And my van isn't taxed or insured. And the trees and walls will be coming down on me, worse than the Flood. And there's one man in the county offices I think might help. I'll try him before I go to the Guards."

"Wait now, Mr Duff." Mr Foley no longer wished to keep Michael talking, for he was thirsting to spread the news. "I'll give you a tip, Mr Duff. For what it's worth. Try dialling the number back to front. Diametrically opposite. I did it once in the last extremity of despair and I was on to me man in a jiffy."

"Good chap." Michael hung up and carried out Mr Foley's suggestion, listening with bated breath as the bell began to ring.

"Hullo there!" said Mr Foley's voice again, now fraught with impatience. "I'll be with you in one min-yoot." The receiver went down with a sharp little click. Michael sank onto a wooden chest, holding his head in his hands.

Tomo came in like a shadow and silently took up the telephone book. Awhile he studied it, then, seating himself on the chest at Michael's side, he took the telephone on his knee and held it firm, he inserted a pencil in one of the dialling sockets and moved it round an inch or so, holding the dial face in its new position with an enormous thumb. Next he took the receiver off and under these awkward conditions gingerly dialled the number, listened impassively as it rang and, passing the instrument to his employer, flitted away as quietly as he had come, to remain within earshot at the front door.

"Good morning. County offices here."

Michael had long ceased to marvel at the fertility of Tomo's resource in all affairs other than those he was paid to carry out. Thankfully he asked for the rate collector and was put through to his friend Mr Collins, who immediately disclaimed any knowledge of that individual's affairs. Mr Duff was only through to him because he chanced to be alone there that morning. The three gentlemen who might conceivably have helped him were all away. Mr Lennox was out sick with an ulcer, Mr Boydell was making a Retreat and Mr Fay was off to the races at Mallow. Having given these organisational details in a tone of modest pride, Mr Collins went on to enquire what Mr Duff's trouble might be and to express the keenest sympathy with him.

"Sure, you'll want to be using the car yourself," he cried. "Did you not tell him that?"

"I never saw the fellow at all," Michael replied. "He was up and away with it while we were at breakfast."

"And never gave you a receipt!" Mr Collins exclaimed. "Now, that's against procedure."

He began to describe the procedure laid down for cases of arrears of rates and to explain that, since it had not been followed, Michael must be mistaken and the car never seized at all. For, Mr Collins affirmed, if there was one thing he and his colleagues were hot on, it was procedure. There was a German the other day now, one of the great new factory owners flooding the country, asked could he leave in his son with them to get a grounding before he went to the Civil Service in Munich. A German! That ought to give Mr Duff an idea of how Ballinaduff managed its affairs. And anyway, he concluded, if indeed such a fearful step had been contemplated, he, Mr. Collins, would have heard something about it for sure.

"But the car's taken, all the same," Michael persisted.

"Taken, ah yes. Not seized."

He was about to clarify this nuance when Michael interrupted him. His experienced mind was gradually piecing the fragments together into an ordered whole as monstrous as it was familiar. "Wait now," he said. "Lennox is ill, Boydell is in cahoots with the Almighty and Fay is making whoopee. Right?"

"Well now, I wouldn't have put it in precisely that kind of a way . . ."

"Has Fay a car of his own?"

A silence followed these words, broken only by a feverish scraping at Mr Collins's stubbly chin.

"Well?" barked the master of Georgetown.

"There are some questions, Mr Duff," then said Mr Collins, finely and sadly, "that no Irish gentleman puts."

"To hell with Irish gentlemen."

"And that no Irish official would answer," Mr Collins went on, as before.

"I can believe you!" Michael banged the receiver down.

"Whom were you talking to, darling?" asked Mrs Duff as she whisked a cobweb from the tiara of Great-aunt Charlotte.

"County offices."

"I thought they only spoke Molly," his mother commented. "That wasn't Molly you were speaking, was it?"

"No. Oh, Mother, do let me think."

"I am not stopping you, dearest boy."

Seething, Michael went out to order the stallion to be saddled. He had not ridden him out for two or three days and the horse was apt to be wicked at any time. A broken arm or some such would about cook his goose altogether at present. But there was no help for it: he had laid up the van for the quarter as an economy and he dared not drive it uninsured.

When Paddy received the order the sheepish look returned to his face at once.

"Well now, what is it, what is it? Don't tell me he was seized as well."

Paddy laughed admiringly, by way of a diversion. "Ah, you're gas all right, Master Michael."

"*What is wrong with Dano, Paddy?*" He fixed a

burning glance on the groom as if the truth could be sucked from him as the sun sucks moisture from the earth.

"He isn't walking so well since yesterday, sir," Paddy said, looking away. "The little bit of his pleasure he took in the garden there did him no good at all."

Dano was lame: that was that. "Could you hitch the asses to the dog cart, then?"

Paddy poured out a flood of reasons why this would be technically impossible. He meant that it would not do for the master of Georgetown to cut a figure of fun driving about the country behind a couple of donkeys: it was unsuitable for Mr Duff, it would reflect on himself and he was not going to allow it.

"There's only one thing left, then," Michael declared. "Start up the Blitz!"

The Blitz was a huge ungainly invalid's chair that thirteen years ago a neighbour had asked the Duffs to house for a week or two. A note almost of frenzy came into the groom's voice as he stated that it would take all day and all night to get the batteries charged. He appealed in his anguish to Tomo, who, supporting him, affirmed that in addition it would undoubtedly blow all the fuses or even send the house up in flames. Before they could go further into the matter, Atracta came to the door and screamed that the telephone was a-shouting. All messages and inquiries had to be bawled from door or window in this way, for she believed her domestic status immeasurably superior to that of the outdoor staff and feared to lower it by physically leaving the shelter of the house. To see her bugling away on the step, her mouth a great black O in her wide pink face, roused Michael to fury.

"Then answer it, you silly old fool!"

"I did, Master Michael, so. I took it up and asked what did ail it, and I laid it down on its side."

"Who was it, then?"

"It asked for yourself, Master Michael dear, it didn't say nothin' personal."

"Oh, Christ! Was it a man or a woman, Atracta?"

Atracta gave him a startled look. "How would I ask it a thing like that, Master Michael?" That's gentry, she reflected: shameless. I'll swing for her one of these days, Michael promised himself: Duff of Georgetown shall end his long line on the gallows. "Out of my sight," he vociferated, striding towards the door. "Don't let me see you again today."

"There's no need in the world to raise your voice, Master Michael honey," Atracta said with dignity and in the consciousness of individual worth. "I'm the last one alive to push meself forward." She disappeared indoors, wondering once more as she went if the young master were not a little sweet on her all the same.

"Darling, how sickening for you about the car." The little voice was both cool and warm, and made him think of cream and honey and velvet and silk and everything else of value or delight.

"Oh, it's you." The tempests raging about him died

down and he was lying becalmed in a patch of sunlight. "Foley didn't lose much time."

It turned out that Mr Foley's turn of speed surpassed his bent for accuracy, for Dulcie was under the impression that tinkers, driving the car to Ballinaduff to sell it there, had smashed it against a tree. On learning the truth she at once offered to come and fetch him in her own veteran motor, when the two of them would set out in pursuit of the miscreant. Although Mr Fay had the start of them, the first race at Mallow was never before half past one and he might well pause along the road to refresh himself. Further, there were only three possible routes to Mallow from Crummagh and friends of hers lived alongside two: these should be instructed forthwith to erect and to man barricades while Michael and herself would set out along the third. She would be with him in half an hour.

Michael thought, what a field marshal was lost to the world when Dulcie agreed to become his wife. "But your pigs! Your hens! Your father!"

"This is an emergency," Dulcie replied with great steadiness.

"Oh! I love emergencies."

"So do I."

Mrs Duff stopped in the act of stroking Grandfather Duff's bemedalled breast to inquire, "Who was that, darling?"

"It was Dulcie, Mother."

"The little Browning girl? Is she still at home?"

(53)

The General received a jab in the solar plexus. "Lucius should get her away to England. Otherwise she will be running off and marrying a groom. And a Catholic groom at that." The General was tapped on the nose for emphasis. Beside him Michael's father was looking down, his face square and strong and faintly amused by something. Old Bob the English sheep dog lay beneath it and thumped the floor with his tail whenever his mistress took a step towards him.

"Mother, Dulcie is going to marry me. You know that very well," Michael said, with anger in his voice: they had this out so often and so often.

"Yes, yes, of course, how stupid I am," she said, confused. "Very suitable, darling, and convenient as well. I must have been thinking of someone else."

In the haggard Paddy and Tomo were both rooted to the ground in consternation, piling up arguments against the use of the Blitz. The instant their employer reappeared they both gave tongue together and remained in full cry long after he had informed them of the change in plan. For the rest of that day, indeed, they continued mechanically to devise, revise and compare their pleas, the impact on their minds having been too severe to pass off lightly. Michael left them at it and went to look at Dano, who was seriously lame in the off hind leg. He sent John in search of remedies and shouted a few instructions to the other two as they stood deep in their litigation. Then he began strolling down the avenue to meet Dulcie, smelling the wet earth and the sappy trees and thinking life not too bad in spite of all. The gale was slackening at last and ragged patches of blue showed here and there between the flying clouds. Buds on the rhododendron bushes were fat and rosy, the branches of the old lime trees were misting over with yellow. The stream was chattering busily away, full to the brim, and the banks were studded with primrose.

At the front gates he waited with the wind ruffling his hair and looked at the wild lovely face of his country. All troubles had retired to the back of his mind. His heart beat fast as the sound of a broken-winded engine was heard and Dulcie's ancient jalopy came panting into view. The sight of her serious little face above the wheel had an effect on him this morning like a match on petrol.

"I've got a wonderful idea!" he exploded, pushing her out of the driver's seat like a bag of corn and placing himself there instead. He took the money out of his pockets and counted it over. "We'll run round for a bit to see what the damage is here. Then we'll drive to the airport for lunch."

"To Shannon, Michael? But the car . . . Mallow . . . Fay . . ."

"Hang Fay," he replied. "This is an emergency. Didn't you say so yourself?" With that he pulled her to him and began methodically and industriously to kiss her.

"One of these days you'll break my nose," she gasped when at last he let her go.

"Never mind, it's a horrid little nose," he said, tweeking it. "And you can always say you did it boxing. People will respect you for it."

"Shannon would be so lovely," Dulcie sighed.

"It will be so lovely."

He laughed and let in the clutch. They set off together with a blithe sense of wrongdoing. Michael had to be told of everything that had happened to her since they met the Sunday before. Yesterday had been terrible; everything had been upside down and the laundry had sent back the wrong evening shirt, an extraordinary thing, all frills, they supposed it might belong to the county manager; and she had rung up several times and couldn't get a single word of sense from any of them. Everyone apparently had been at Mass! Why should they have gone to Mass?

"It was a first Friday," Michael told her, as one steeped in tribal lore.

"But, Michael, first of what?"

"I was afraid you might ask that. I haven't the foggiest," he admitted.

"I wish this celebrated Faith of theirs included things like telling the truth or keeping their word or even getting the laundry right," complained Dulcie.

"But then they would never have clung to it through the centuries."

It had been particularly unfortunate about the shirt because Mr Browning only had two of them and the other was in the laundry basket. That evening he was to read a paper on Diderot to the Ballinaduff Philosophical Society and if he could not go there dressed as a gentleman, he said, he would not go at all. In the end they got his shirt for him but not before their nerves were worn to a frazzle. Dahlia the sow was in pig again. And they had killed a pig on the Wednesday and the bacon had gone off to be cured and the sausages were a poem. They would have loin of pork tomorrow. The gardener, aged sixty-five, was looking for a wife, and not just any old reactor either: young and handsome, the aspirants were required to be, good cooks and with money in the bank. A Jehovah's Witness had called and kept her talking about Judgment Day for thirty-seven minutes, with his foot in the door like a gypsy.

"How dared he!" Michael said, fuming.

And what was Michael's own news?

"I've sacked Atracta!" he cried. "She is to go at the end of the month."

"What a capital idea!" Dulcie looked at him fondly. "And only think—Papa has decided to give up being an eighteenth-century man of letters and attend to the farm."

"How dare you make fun of me? Wait until we are married," he told her gravely. "This time it is true. The wind of change is blowing. I have proclaimed myself a republic."

"Oh, Michael, you are potty and no mistake!"

"Better so. Better so."

A band of blue had appeared across the horizon and

was steadily widening, sweeping the clouds before it as it advanced. The country wore a beaming innocent smile as if it were saying, "*Gales*, are you mad? We don't have gales in Ireland." The damage of the night before was roughly what Michael had expected it to be. A heavy gate was blown off its hinges, thirty-three trees were down, one of them blocking the lane that the tractor had to use, a stack of straw had been evenly spread over the field round it and Mrs Dooley declared she could count the blessed stars through the holes in her roof. It only strengthened Michael's resolve to enjoy himself with Dulcie this one day if it was the last thing he ever did.

"I'm going to have that gooey pie and salad," she said, as they swung out on to the Limerick road beyond Crummagh. "And a cream meringue. It is ages since I had cream meringue. Is there money for cream meringue?"

"If we don't have anything to start with. I'm going to have steak and onions and fried potatoes."

"You always do. I never remember you having anything else."

"Try living on what Atracta sends up, and you'll know what starvation means. Never mind, she'll soon be gone."

Then Dulcie had to hear the whole tale of Atracta's nineteenth or was it twentieth dismissal, with what she had said and Michael had said, and how she had taken it and how she had been since. "But will she go?" was her query when the recital was done.

"I tell you I've sacked her. Don't you understand."

"Ah."

"What do you mean, Ah? I'll give you Ah. Ah indeed, you're worse than mother."

This morning the tinkers were out on the road in force, moving east in round, gaily painted wagons with skewbald horses trotting riderless and at large in their rear. Michael drove with care and slowed down at every turn in deference to the tinker habit of debouching onto a main road as if no one but themselves had ever thought of using it. Up one of the moorland lanes that came meandering down a steepish hill he caught sight of what looked like a tinker encampment. Two vehicles were heeling over at a drunken angle in the ditches, one on each side, and the roadway was strewn with a variety of articles. Then he looked again and realized that this state of affairs was unintentional, and with a groan pulled up.

"Looks like a spill," he said. "Botheration! I suppose we should go and help."

"I suppose so," Dulcie said without enthusiasm.

Michael backed and turned up the lane, and his hawk's eye pounced on another and more arresting detail. "Dulcie! But isn't that my car?" he shouted. "I swear it's my car."

He drove to the spot, wildly accelerating. It was

indeed a curious spectacle that offered itself to their contemplation. To begin with, this accident should never have taken place. The stolen car had been coming down the hill and the other vehicle, a travelling hardware van, had been going up, and there was ample room for them to pass each other by. At the psychological moment, it seemed, an overpowering mutual aversion had caused them both to swerve and now they were both soundly ditched. One man was doubled over the wheel of Michael's car asleep, while another, in his shirt sleeves and crimson in the face with exertion, was collecting the kettles, buckets, brushes and bars of soap and arranging them haphazardly in little piles.

"There's a rope in the back," Dulcie said, as Michael pulled up and leaped out. She had sensed all along that the day would end in haulage.

"It oughtn't to be allowed," the man in shirt sleeves said. "It's a national disgrace." Frowning, he ambled away to pick up a frying pan.

Michael experienced the old old feeling of living out his life in a bad and interminable farce. "That's my car and it's stolen," he said. "Would you lend a hand till I lift the fellow out of it?"

"Drink!" the man in shirt sleeves continued censoriously, paying no heed to Michael's request. "The curse of the country." He scoured the pan with his elbow, polished it on the seat of his trousers and replaced it in the puddle where it had been lying.

It was all so amusing, so enchanting, so charmingly

crazy and original and poetic and different. "Say, Elmer!"
Michael had once overheard a tourist exclaim to her husband. "Why don't we just settle here, in this lovely place,
among all these lovely people?" *Say, Elmer!* had been a
code word of his and Dulcie's ever since. Boiling with
rage he flung open the door of his car, dragged Mr Fay
from the seat and dumped him on the marshy ground.
Mr Fay stirred and moaned in his sleep but gave no
other sign of life.

"Won't you help me tip this back on the road?"
Michael again begged the advocate of enforced temper-
ance.

The man desisted at last from his occupation and
walked slowly and uncertainly towards the newcomers.
Beads of sweat hung thick on his flaming brow and there
was a look in his eye as if he were not altogether among
those present. "Degrading themselves to the level of
brute creation!" he resumed. "Holy Ireland, how are
you!"

"Oh, do give me a hand here, there's a great
fellow."

"Ah, it's a grand way all right," cried the man in
sudden bitterness, pointing one comminatory finger at
the unconscious Fay, "to be celebrating the birth of Our
Blessed Lord!"

"He imagines it's Christmas," Michael said to Dulcie
in a despairing manner.

"Why, it's not even Easter," Dulcie said, looking
at the man severely.

The pair of them broke down all at once. Leaning against the bonnet of the car they laughed and laughed amid the ruins of their day and the hopelessness of their lives, laughed in wild voluptuous peals until the tears stood in their eyes. The man in his shirt sleeves gazed at one and then at the other in bewilderment. He wore the air of one who ever found the world mysterious and now, with more new fantastic and unheard-of addendum to his information, knows it to lie forever beyond his grasp. Very slowly, and as it were carefully, his legs buckled and gave way, depositing him on the ground. There he reclined, his crimson face turned up to the now blue and tender sky in an agony of interrogation.

Michael tried to pull himself together. "Say, Elmer!" he feebly began, whereat they both broke down again. At last he recovered sufficiently to seize her in his arms and they clung to each other in a mingling of desperation and bliss. "Dulcie Dulcie Dulcie," he murmured, kissing her as if he never meant to stop, all over her face and her hair and her neck and the little brown washing cooking dusting gardening hand that wore his ring.

A croak like that of a startled frog came from somewhere on the ground near by. Mr Fay had managed to get one eye open and, propped on his elbow, was malevolently surveying them with it. It was clear that he had something of importance to say but could not, for reasons beyond his control: his mouth opened and shut and opened and shut, or by way of variation slipped sidewise, but no message proceeded from it. This confrontation of spirit with flesh had an element of grandeur in it, seeming to speak of humanity at its noblest and most exalted and, as befitted, after a long determined struggle the spirit prevailed.

"I saw yous," Mr Fay opened fire, articulating as if his tongue had turned into a rubber ball. "I saw the pair of yous, there. A fine way all right for Christians to conduct themselves. And on the open road. The way you'd skangle . . . dankle . . . scandalize any decent Christian that happened to pass. It's things like that get the country a bad name."

With that he allowed the eye to close again and, gratefully sinking back to the horizontal position, took his ease.

Five

THE early part of Sunday morning went by in a rush that was little short of a panic. Michael rose with the lark and did essential jobs until the men looked in for an hour or so after Mass. When they came up the avenue one by one in their black suits, walking slowly and stiffly as if weights hung on their ankles, he ran to wash and dress and drive his mother to their own parish church, fifteen miles away; and after that, drive her home again and himself over to Rougemain, where Dulcie Browning lived. Rougemain was a short three miles from St George's but Mrs Duff, although included in the Sunday invitations, invariably thought of some reason why she could not go, and invariably, therefore, Michael had the double journey to make.

He got the car out now and sat in it under her

window, hooting in impatience. The vehicle bore the marks of its recent adventure, a badly scratched bonnet, a buckled mudguard, a pervasive composite smell inside and a medal of St Christopher abandoned on the floor. "Hurry, Mother, do. We shall be late." They were nearly always late.

"Lucius keeps up wonderfully," Mrs Duff remarked as she settled herself beside him, a motoring veil tied over her hat in the style of 1910. "It would be so delightful to see him again. Will he be there today, should you think?"

Mr Browning never set foot in a church, in accordance with the spirit of eighteenth-century enlightenment, but Mrs Duff put this question every week.

"No, Mother. How many times have I told you? He doesn't believe in God."

"That has nothing whatever to do with it, darling," Mrs Duff responded. "I have told *you* so quite a number of times. And I very much want to see him."

"Then you must come to Rougemain," Michael said absently. He had just noted another ominous bulge in his wall where it might be expected to collapse without too much delay.

"I should have liked it immensely!" she exclaimed. "But I must write to those Sinn Feiners about my parcel. Michael, what an extraordinary smell. Do you think a fox can have got into the car?"

"No. It's just dirty clothes and Guinness."

"You look quite clean to me," his mother said, surveying him with pride. "But I wish you wouldn't drink that stuff. It would never have passed your father's lips. Promise me not to do it again, like a dear boy, at any rate not before church. I remember the time a fox got into Ballysimon's carriage, it had to be laid by for weeks, the smell was so dreadful. The old lady was still alive at the time. I think that is what has really happened today. You are perfectly clean, and I cannot imagine a Duff drinking stout in the morning." Satisfied, she allowed the matter to drop.

As usual, the service had begun when they got to the old grey lichened church of St George. The congregation here consisted week after week of the same few people, all well known to each other and most of them in some way or another related, dotted about in an edifice a hundred times too large. They sat meditating on their private affairs in high wooden pews, under tattered regimental flags, beside Grecian burial urns inscribed with appropriate sentiments in elegant Latin: the form of service, by way of reaction from the idolatries practised all around, was extremely low. Dulcie was there, wearing the blue tweeds that Michael had given her, with her leggy younger sister Anne Louise. The Master of Foxhounds was arrayed in a fur coat and velvet toque which looked strange on her and faintly improper. His lean blue jaws working as he ceaselessly ground his teeth, Kilrany of Kilrany, the only other man under sixty, turned a look of sardonic commiseration on Michael as he bustled his mother down the aisle. There were the colonels, the majors, the captains and their consorts; a doctor and his wife; and a poor widow woman with four children, who had embraced the Protestant faith after an altercation with Father Murphy and who dismayed the other worshippers by the vulgar brio of their hymn singing.

The Rector, Canon Bilkin, was a frail old man, so tired that he could scarcely hold up his head. He often and piteously begged for leave to retire but Kilrany would not hear of it, saying that he must go on until he dropped like everyone else. This morning he preached in his sad whisper on the encumbrance of material possessions and the vanity of high estate. Lulled by the sound of it Michael dozed off, while Kilrany's maxillas worked on and on like pistons. Afterwards he came across to the Duffs as they prepared to drive home.

"Morning, Aunt Virginia. Morning, Michael. Hope you profited by the sermon," he said grimly. Kilrany always followed the sermon, to the amusement of everyone else. "I know I did. I'm making my overdraft and mortgages over to the poor tomorrow. Michael, how does your place look after the little breath of fresh air yesterday?"

"Pretty frightful, thank you. And a wall came down before that."

Kilrany shuddered. "Don't talk to me about walls," he snarled, and stamped off without another word.

"When I was a girl, young men were expected to make themselves agreeable," Mrs Duff said plaintively, looking at the retreating landowner.

Michael laughed. "Hugh is all right, really." Kilrany was about the only young man in the whole of Ireland that he did not envy.

He left his mother at home, promising not to stay too long away, and took the road again for Rougemain with leaping heart. It was a beautiful sunny morning, as if the elements were sorry for their pranks of the day before and were trying to make amends. The country had never looked better than now in the fresh green and brilliant yellow of spring with the far-off hills changing from brown to blue to purple in the soft western light. At Rougemain the door stood open wide in welcome and Bicky the terrier flung himself on the visitor, yelping with joy. Bridget was in the hall, a decent bonny smiling countrywoman, in such poignant contrast to Atracta that Michael could never see her without a stab of envy. Both he and his mother had long admired and coveted this pearl among women: indeed, Mrs Duff went so far as to say she must have gentle blood in her, it being her fixed belief that excellence in the lower orders could only arise through the sexual lapse of a forbear. Bridget greeted Michael now, said that Miss Dulcie was occupied in the kitchen and that the master was expecting him in the library. He was, Bridget said, lowering her voice respectfully, arranging his papers.

Mr Browning was at a round table by the window,

his serene white brow puckered a little in thought and a number of cardboard files spread out before him. The youngest of five boys, he had never dreamed that the estate would be his and from an early age had cultivated an interest in the higher thought and a scorn for the Irish landed gentry and all their occupations. The two eldest brothers were killed within a week of arriving in France for the first world war, the next died of drink ten years later and the fourth broke his neck in the hunting field. Mr Browning became master of Rougemain as he had always secretly longed to do, but too late: by then he was imprisoned in his attitudes and indeed, through sheer lack of information, had come to look on himself as a man of uncommon intellect. He was now aged fifty-odd years, with not a grey hair in his head and the slim lithe figure of a boy. His face was heart-shaped like Dulcie's and he had the same charming smile, a smile which appeared in full fig as Michael stood and hesitated on the threshold.

"My dear boy, how delightful to see you," he said, jumping up. "And how very kind you are, to have come all this way to see an old man like me. Sit down and have a glass of sherry before luncheon."

" 'Lo, Michael," muttered Anne Louise, without looking up. She lay sprawled on her stomach on the hearth rug, reading Surtees.

"I think your greeting might have been more elaborate," her father remarked, moving towards the sherry decanter with elastic tread. "You will not be able to come into this room if you behave like a savage." There was no reply. "This child is such a disappointment," Mr Browning remarked with rueful humour, as he did every time he saw Michael and always in the child's presence. "I did hope one of them might share my interests. Dulcie has nothing in her head but pigs and hens and cookery; and this one, although named after Madame de Staël, thinks of nothing in life but hunting!"

"What else is there in life to think about?" the Disappointment growled.

"She will be in a coma now all through summer, until it starts again," her parent continued, ignoring the interruption. "Ah Michael, thank your good fortune that you are not a father."

"But I hope to be, one of these days," Michael reminded him, sitting down.

"You are not serious!" Mr Browning exclaimed. He greatly disliked the idea of Dulcie engaged to anyone at all as being sure to affect his comfort and convenience, and when Mr Browning disliked anything he was wont to pretend it was not there.

"But I am. Very serious indeed." The old anger crept into his voice in spite of himself.

"No, no, no." Mr Browning indulgently waved these fancies aside. "You are much better off as you are, my dear young friend: take it from me." He began to pour out the sherry in a special way he had, putting a teaspoonful or so in the bottom of the glass and then adding drops one by one, like a cook dripping oil into

mayonnaise, until it reached a quarter of the way up.
"Now! I'm very fond of a glass of sherry. A civilized
drink, at all events. Well, how was Mr Tompkins?" Mr
Tompkins was the name he bestowed on the Deity. "I am
always surprised that grown people should continue to
believe in him, let alone avow it in public. They would
presumably hesitate to confess to a belief in fairies or
Father Christmas: although I have known ladies to do
both." There was a pause in the conversation while Mr
Browning helped himself to sherry, freely. "I have been
enjoyably busy all the morning," he went on. "In the
strange lighthouse existence I lead I cannot keep in touch
with other minds except by constant correspondence:
all of which has to be carefully sorted and filed if I am
not to lose track of it." Mr Browning picked up a post
card with a few words of writing on one side and waved
it as a banner. "Now, this is someone I daresay you never
heard of," he said, beaming. "None other than the great
Morenius of Bonn. A mind that towers above almost all
others in the world today. I had written querying a point
in his last great work and here is his reply. 'Sehr freund-
lich. Aber nicht Heidegger sondern Hegel wurde in
dieser Beziehung zitiert. Hochachtung." Mr Browning
pronounced the German words unnecessarily well. "Forgive me," he caught himself up, "I should have translated.
'Very kind. Not Heidegger, however, but Hegel was
quoted in this connection. Yours faithfully.' Clear,
Michael, lapidary and clear! A translucent mind. To be
candid, I have forgotten just what point it was I raised.

But his answer came almost by return of post." Mr Browning carefully filed the card away again among dozens of other perfunctory acknowledgments, and took a pull at his sherry.

"I hope you had a successful evening at Ballinaduff on Friday," Michael remembered to ask.

The glow faded from the philosopher's face and a look of weary disgust came over it. "The lights went out in the middle," he said bitterly. "I was just reading about the Illumination: there was something symbolic in that sudden darkness. And you heard, of course, the story of my shirt? Sometimes I wonder why I struggle on."

There was a giggle from the hearth rug, this being the Disappointment's reaction to Mr Jorrocks being shot head first into a watery ditch; and Mr Browning's face and voice underwent a complete transformation.

"Anne Louise!" he shrilled.

"Oh, what is it now?" she groaned.

"I do not expect you to laugh if I am annoyed or inconvenienced."

"I wasn't! I didn't! Wasn't listening, so there!"

"I expect you to listen while I am speaking."

"You were talking to Michael, I thought."

"Don't answer me back, girl. And put that book away at once. You are not to open it again today. If you insist on reading muck you shall not read at all."

Off already, Michael thought in exasperation; but at that moment Dulcie came in to say that luncheon was on the table and he bounded up from his chair like a yacht whose sails catch a sudden breeze.

Mr Browning recovered himself at once. "Anne Louise will have her meal in the kitchen," he said, with his enchanting smile. "The servants' conversation will be very much to her taste. And I shall not have to blush for her in front of my visitor."

The child burst into tears and flung out of the room.

"Oh, Father. On Sunday." Dulcie put a tired hand to her forehead.

"My dear girl," Mr Browning replied with a light laugh, "to me, I'm afraid, Sunday is the day when break-fast is cold and there is no coffee at eleven. Indeed," he observed to Michael, "you may say that I have a calendar all of my own. Christmas is when my younger daughter eats herself sick and my poor wife's Aunt Edwina comes for a fortnight and sits in my chair. Easter is marked by the good Rector, for obscure sentimental reasons of his own, dragging himself up here to call, and by flowers mysteriously vanishing from my garden to adorn the native temples. At Whitsun the hideous heirs of the English industrial revolution crowd the banks of my streams to steal my fish, communicating with each other by sounds barely human. And so on. Throughout the Christian year, each festival for me has its own dread connotation." He led the way to the dining room, chuckling.

"Your hair looks like gold," Michael said to Dulcie as a ray of sun fell across her head.

"She has it, of course, from me," Mr Browning said, carving the joint on the sideboard. "I wonder if like mine it will keep its colour. Her poor mother, as you may know, was completely grey by the time she was thirty-three."

"Dan, you must serve on the left-hand side," Dulcie said, as, breathing heavily, the boy bore down on them with a plate in either huge hand. Mr Browning insisted that he should be waited on at table by a male, one of the last little elegances he clung to in a vulgar age. "Goodness, I'm tired of telling you."

"And isn't this the left, then, Miss Dulcie?" the lad inquired, turning scarlet.

"It is not."

"Abysmal," said Mr Browning.

Dan meekly went round to the other side but his self-confidence was undermined. Bringing the vegetable dishes to the table he somehow managed to get his wrists crossed and in the attempt to disentangle them dropped the potatoes on the floor. Petrified, he stood and gazed at the steaming pile with his mouth open.

"All right, Dan, you may go," Dulcie murmured, and gratefully he took to his heels.

"There was a time when he would have been soundly whipped for that," Mr Browning observed, in the wistful tone he used for making such statements. Having taken his place at the head of the table he leaned back and folded his hands with an air of exaggerated patience.

(74)

"Well, you won't have Bridget," Dulcie called from the floor, where she was salvaging what she could of the potatoes.

"Let me," Michael said, springing up as she made ready to wait on them herself.

"I begin to feel giddy," Mr Browning complained. "Perhaps, Michael, you would sit down again and allow Dulcie to look after us. She is a good little soul."

"Isn't she!"

"In fact she has only one real fault," her father went on, helping himself to claret and omitting to pass the decanter. "She declines to copy my manuscripts. And she has such a clear neat hand!"

"One must draw the line," Dulcie said, offering him applesauce.

"Must one, my dear, indeed? Then I wonder where." The smile shone out again. "The Countess Tolstoy copied the whole of *War and Peace* by hand seven times over."

"But that was a masterpiece," Michael commented.

The smile vanished. "Possibly, very possibly," Mr Browning said. "I think it overrated. I have never gone in for novel reading, an occupation rather more appropriate to the ladies, bless them, than to a man of intellect. Nevertheless, I have made exceptions now and again. *Wuthering Heights, Middlemarch, David Copperfield, War and Peace, Madame Bovary* . . . They have all struck me as a good deal of fuss about nothing."

"I never get time for reading," Michael said.

(75)

The meal dragged uncomfortably on. The philosopher withdrew into himself, staring into space as if he were alone and starting a little if either of them spoke. Directly he had finished eating he went away. It had been his intention to take Michael with him to the library and read him the paper on Diderot; but he now decided against it, as a punishment for the young man's want of tact. How strange a quirk of Fate, he mused, as he often did, to have set him, Lucius Browning, in a misty boggy island on the rim of the world surrounded with Yahoos, bosthoons and a mindless squirearchy!

The lovers thought they were going to have the afternoon to themselves. They would harness The Walnut to the trap and drive through the lanes and woods round about, a treat that Dulcie loved and could seldom enjoy in the winter, when the sagacious and versatile Walnut was out every hunting day with Anne Louise. But when they went to the paddock to catch the pony they found the child already there, her arms round his neck, her face buried in his mane, in a state of such misery that they had to invite her to join them. They drove about for an hour or so, talking of dull things or of nothing. Then Michael began to worry about his mother, alone at Georgetown and up to heaven knew what, for she made her displeasure at his engagement felt in all manner of ingenious ways. It was like that most Sundays: pressures without, tensions within, tugged at from every side, moidered by all. They came silently home.

"You'll come to the Hunt Ball?" Michael said as he

got into his car again, dragging one more empty afternoon with him.

"Indeed I will not. I've nothing at all to wear."

"Come naked then," Michael advised her. "We'll make 'em all sit up. Goodbye, darling. Goodbye, Clip-Clop."

Mrs Duff was lying stretched out on a sofa in the drawing room, her face a deadly white and her eyes closed. She had tripped and fallen over a dustpan left at the head of the stairs, plumb in the middle of the top stair. It was placed where she could not help but fall over it and must have been deliberately put there. An attempt had been made on her life, the marvel was that no one had made it before. Old Bob had been uneasy all the afternoon and it was probable that the assassins were still lurking near at hand: Michael must take his revolver like a dear good boy and examine the rooms of Georgetown one by one.

"And the shrubbery," she concluded.

"It was Atracta, Mother. Everything in the house is Atracta."

Mrs Duff opened her eyes and looked at him as if he had not spoken. Then she launched into a recital of the whole affair again and repeated her interpretation of it, this time tracing a connection between the dustpan on the stairs and the fox in the motor car. The fox in Ballysimon's carriage, now that she came to think of it, had been a fishy business too, never properly explained. "It's all bound up with this question of the parcel and the straw," she told her son. "Please do search the house and the shrubbery, darling boy, I shan't rest until you have done it. And be sure to take your revolver."

There was no choice then but to set out on a tour of the thirty-four musty dusty cobwebbed rooms of Georgetown, lugubrious with their sheeted chairs and tables and draped pictures and chandeliers, and the ragged overgrown shrubberies behind the house. How pleasant, he thought as he marched along the creaking boards, to come in fact on a bunch of desperadoes! Without hesitating he would throw wide his arms and call "Shoot!" But there was nobody at all: he met no living creature other than the hosts of spiders, and rats and one sleepy little brown owl; no one had passed that way for a long time and the glaze of dust was smooth as newly fallen snow.

His mother was watching a film of bird life on the television when he came into the drawing room again and, when he attempted to speak to her, held up a hand in protest.

"Do let's have a little peace now, darling boy," she said. "We seem to have had no peace all day."

Six

SUNDAY was over and Monday was back again already: once spring had begun the weeks sped by with gathering momentum, like a merry-go-round in a fair, while the pattern of each day was fixed and unaltering. Over Monday morning there always hung the shadow of Tomo, who spent the whole of the day and much of the night before drinking alone in his cottage. Sometimes he was still unconscious at sunrise and did not come to work at all. Then his duties were shared between Paddy and John, who glowered for the rest of the day. At other times he arrived so drunk he could hardly stand, and would go to ground in a corner of the barn at the first opportunity. He would choose out a lair with patient, inebriate cunning, burrow furtively down in the hay until he was buried and out of sight, and then notify the world of his whereabouts with a snore like a clap of thunder. Now and again he would hurt himself, cut his head or fall on the fire, and go to hospital to be patched up; and an odd time he would break out and the Guards would take him in, and he would have to be fetched from the courthouse and the fine paid. Nothing could get underway on Monday until his condition had been ascertained.

This morning he had turned up on the stroke of his hour, had at once occupied himself with the cows and at present was leading the bull out to pasture. Such was the account that Paddy gave Michael, whose spirits rose with a rush. It seemed like an omen: this was one of the days when for no particular reason he felt glad to be alive and brimmed over with energy and the wish to work: he was going to drag the fallen tree off the tractor's lane single-handed, he would order slates for the roofs, he would study the wall again and think what could be done, and all before lunch. He was ready and able for anything and anyone.

Mrs Duff was at the breakfast table before him. A pile of correspondence left over from Saturday lay on the sideboard and, looking unusually alert, she read in a letter fished out at random.

"Michael! Young Buchanan is to come home," she opened fire the instant he appeared. "To live. Did you ever hear of such a thing?"

"Good Lord, he isn't! Nothing wrong with the old man, is there?" Michael could not think that one who had broken through the net would return unless for illness or death.

"He's not going to Mount Mellin at all," Mrs Duff replied, waving the letter. "He's going to set up in Ballinaduff! And to practise law! Poor Julia."

Michael remembered Roger Buchanan's calm owlish face and the eternal enthusiasms and excitements bubbling away behind it. "He was always cracky," he pointed out, smiling. "Think of that marriage of his."

"Oh, that," Mrs Duff said, waving it aside. "People always make things out worse than they are. I don't suppose he was properly married at all. But this is terrible. It appears that he's gone Celtic over there in London, and learned to speak Molly. And Julia, poor thing, says that from the way he writes he seems to have turned republican. Surely, Michael," quavered Mrs Duff, "he would be better dead?"

"I suppose he'll chuck it, once he's here," Michael soothed her.

"Depend upon it, he will end in the Dail. And who will speak to him? Tell me that. Attorneys, dentists, auctioneers. . . ."

"I will, for one," Michael told her gaily. It delighted him to see his mother revive under the stimulus of social disaster. "And if he's any good he shall have our business. He's one of us, after all. I have to sit up all night to get the better of Ned Mulally, and he's meant to be on my side!"

"One of us!" gravely echoed Mrs Duff. "If I were

not sure of Julia Buchanan I would be sadly inclined to doubt it. If it comes to that there's a drop of bad blood on the old man's side and blood will out, sooner or later." She related in copious and lucid detail the history of a Buchanan's runaway match with a corn chandler's daughter from Ipswich, which had taken place two hundred and fourteen years ago and must, in her view, have given rise to the Celtic and republican sympathies of the present heir. "There is always a reason for things of that sort," she concluded. "One has only to look far enough back."

"I warn you, he'll be asked to join the Under Ninety Club," Michael teased her. "Hugh was saying only the other day we should get a third, to give casting votes and so on. And if it comes to that, I'm a republic too. I declared it on the first day of Friday."

"Certain things are not to be joked about," his mother replied, raising her eyebrows.

Atracta burst into the room a-quiver with importance and indignation and planted herself opposite Michael with arms akimbo. "If you please then," she began, "I can't get the kitchen stove lighting at all."

The sight of the wretch took the cream off his April morning happiness: he pined to hurl the teapot or the toast rack, or both, at her. Angrily he inquired what was wrong with the stove that she couldn't light it after all these years and why did she come peloothering him about it anyway: let her go to the kitchen again and rootle and brackle the culprit until it came to its senses.

"Bedad, then, Master Michael, I can't get near the bloody thing!" This language proved that she felt herself in a strong position. She would have liked to be interrogated further, to maintain the suspense for the grand feeling of power it gave her, but under the glare of Michael's eye she forewent the pleasure. "The great bull does be kneeling in front of it there, as sedate as the ox be the Holy Crib, and he with his poor old head on the turf."

A hush followed these words. Presently Michael rose and at a well-nigh theatrically deliberate pace went to the kitchen. All that startled him there was to learn that Atracta had spoken the truth. The great Hereford bull was kneeling as in her description, exact to the last detail. There was evidence that he had been in the room for some time. His attendant Tomo sprawled in a chair beside the table, his eyes set in his fiery face, and the snivelling triplets perched on the oak dresser, clinging for support to the shelves from which, now and then, a plate or a cup fell to the ground like fruit from a shaken tree. In a way it might have been thought a curious, even an outlandish, interior scene; but taken in context, in its relation to life as Michael knew it, it breathed out the matter-of-fact conventional quality of an old Dutch painting.

Tomo had fully intended to lead the bull to grass but his brain hummed, his eyeballs burned and his tongue was no more good to him than a dried mushroom. He determined to knock on the scullery door and ask Atracta for a cure. It would never have occurred to him to do such a thing if he had been sober, for there was an old hostility between the two, due to the failure of each to admit the spiritual and social superiority of the other. Atracta said haughtily she had nothing for him: there was not a blessed drop to drink in the house, the master was that terrible mean. Unable to conceive of a house without a drop in it, Tomo had lurched forward through the scullery door, pulling the bull behind him and driving Atracta before, in the hope of at any rate scaring a bottle of stout from her. Atracta retreated backwards into the kitchen, followed by her dreadful visitors and shrieking at Heaven, the saints, the triplets and Master Michael to bear out the truth of her words. By the time that Tomo gave it up and prepared to withdraw, the bull had for some reason taken a fancy to his surroundings and declined to leave them. He had gone fussing round and round the kitchen, snorting and drooling, whisking his tail and trying his horns, until all of a sudden he sank on his knees by the range and dozed lightly off.

Michael was unaware of these facts and did not seek to find them out. He would deal with the situation, infuriating as it was, rather than waste time probing into its back history. The first thing he had learned on taking over the estate was that all attempts to uncover the facts behind any outrage whatsoever were not only vain but left the inquirer with a peculiar sensation in his head, as if a lot of bells were ringing there at once. "Come on, damn you," he said, shaking Tomo roughly. "First thing is, to get him out of this." He seized the bull's halter in one hand and a horn in the other, while Tomo staggered up and grasped the tail, looking bewildered and sheepish.

"I'm terrible sorry, sir," he muttered thickly, before he could stop himself.

"And well you might be."

They had a difficult job before them. By now the bull had planned his morning out even as Michael had planned his own, and he was equally vexed by the interruption. He knelt firmly there, relying on his twelve hundred pounds of flesh and bone to carry him through, while his owner and Tomo tugged and prodded and cursed to no avail.

"You should have let me ring him, all the same," Tomo said in a tone of higher wisdom. After his momentary deflation, caused by shock, he felt a pressing need to recover his self-esteem. All critical comment struck him as an insult, and never more so than when justified, so that he was already growing angry with his employer for speaking as he had, and, to make matters worse, in front of the foolish woman.

"I'll have no ringing of bulls," Michael said, panting.

"And how will we ever get him out of this, without?" Tomo demanded, in tipsy triumph. "You could have thought of that, sir, when you wouldn't have it done."

"You are right, of course," Michael snapped back.

"I should have foreseen your doing this bloody-fool thing one day or another." His face lit with a grim smile as he thought how shocked his English cousin would be to hear him talk thus to a servant: dear Cousin Nathaniel with the nice woolly ideas about everything, who asked waiters if they would "mind" bringing him the menu and "believed in" the working class! Sometimes, although it was a horrible thing to wish anyone, Michael would have liked to see him owner of Georgetown and employer of its staff.

Tomo noted the smile, interpreting it as a sneer at himself. "Ah, wait now, sir!" he cried in bitterness. "Wasn't the bull shaping to attack Mrs Smith? And didn't I folly him in here, only to save herself and the young ones?"

"'Tis true for him," Atracta put in, loath to hear falsehood spoken without lending it support.

"A likely tale! Come on now, Tomo, give him one for himself."

After a long and savage tussle the bull resignedly got to his feet, scaling the ample proportions of the kitchen down with his splendid body. Michael thrust the halter into Tomo's shaking hand and, with a final belt on the bull's flank, bade the pair of them speed to the devil. "And no more clowning this day, d'you hear?" he commanded. "You're the worst on the place; and that's not a thing I'd say lightly."

Tomo stumbled out of the kitchen and through the scullery, muttering aggrievedly under his breath. Later on in the day, giving a garbled account of the scene to Paddy and John, he delicately changed the young master's closing remark to "nearly as bad as thim other two," causing both to seethe with fury as well.

"Did you smell the drink on him, the creature?" Atracta whispered with an air of satisfaction, as she lifted her progeny down and bade them go play out of doors, the way they wouldn't dirty their boots. "Ah, God love him, I suppose he'd have to. 'Twill be lonesome there all right, in the poor little cabin, and not a Christian to say a word to him . . ."

Michael cut her short. "I'll send one of the others in to clean this up," he said. "Now tell me, what have you done about Bridie?"

A look of wonder came into the yellow eyes. "Nothing at all, Master Michael, sir," she replied. "Sure, what would I do?"

He saw with despair that his instructions had lost themselves forever in the drifting fogs of her mind. Ridding himself of this woman was going to be a labour akin to cleaning a wall of old ivy. A friend of the family, similarly placed, had cracked the nut by shutting her house for good and removing to Zanzibar; but Michael was not a free man and in any event Atracta and her brood would surely hunt him to the ends of the earth, the Eumenides in frightful modern dress.

"Well, have you begun to look for another place?" he asked.

"God bless you, honey, I have not!" she exclaimed

with fervour. "Is it leave yourself and the dear mistress?"

"Oh, Atracta!" he stormed. "What did I say to you on Friday?"

"On Friday?" Atracta failed to see how anything said on Friday could still be relevant on Monday morning. "You were giving out, Master Michael, tellin' me of me faults and that."

Seeing the lovely ragged blue mountains through the window behind her, Michael wondered for the thousandth time how the Creator had come to give such a land to such a people. He would have liked to rush away into the open air and actually took a step or two towards the door. But how am I ever to gain independence at this rate? he reflected: thinking of the brave resolute Africans, he turned back. "I told you once and for all that you would have to leave us," he said, drawing his strong dark brows together. "Don't dare pretend you've forgotten."

"But I didn't mind you, Master Michael, acushla, not the least little bit in the world," she cried, loving him absolutely.

"You have to go at the end of the month," he told her, very slowly and distinctly. "Let me hear you say it yourself."

"You have to go at the end of the month, Master Michael, honey."

He shot a glance at her, looking for insolence, but there was none, there was nothing but a blank like the broad open sky. "Find yourself something immediately, like a wise woman," he warned her. "From the first of May you won't be employed here. And I'm going for Bridie myself, today."

At the mention of Bridie there was again the sparking of the yellow eyes, which again faded out at once. Atracta hung her head as she had done before and said, "Whatever you like now, Master Michael dear. I wouldn't meself have thought of Bridie for Georgetown, she's that unkempt, but 'tis you are the boss."

"I'm glad you realize that," Michael said with a frown. He had never felt less sure of anything. "And mind there'll be no nonsense when Bridie is here. You must show her round and help her until she finds her feet."

" 'Twill likely be the first time she set them in a gentleman's house," Atracta agreed in a motherly tone.

"More likely be the last time you'll set yours there," and Michael stalked away.

It was ten minutes past eleven. Once more a great bite had been taken out of a working day by sheer tomfoolery. Time seeped away in this country like water taken up the hand. He got chains and tools for work on the fallen tree and started down the avenue in the tractor, only to meet the Master's groom coming up on a bicycle. It appeared that a vixen had her cubs on Michael's land, in an earth near the river where there was danger of them all being drowned if the water rose higher. The Master sent her compliments and had Mr

Duff any objection to their being dug out and removed to a place of safety? For the shortage of foxes was already a matter of grave concern to thinking members of the Hunt. Of course Mr Duff had no objection. What was more, Mr Duff directly renounced all idea of moving that tree that morning or doing any useful work whatever, and came along with the groom to see the fun. The earth was below a clump of elder in a ditch that was steadily filling and an assortment of people were wading and splashing around, giving each other advice. There was the Master in supreme command and finely oblivious of the water covering her ankles, and her friend, the Master of a Pack in the east, with a face like a spade and grizzled bobbed hair: these two ladies between them did the manual work. Old Canon Blessington, from the neighbouring parish, was there to place the fruits of seventy years' experience at their disposal, supplemented incoherently by Mickey Finn, freed from gaol a fortnight earlier and still giddy from the celebration: there was a uniformed nurse, who frequently remarked with a pleasant laugh that her patient would think she had died: two barefoot boys, a Lakeland terrier, a Wicklow collie and a local auctioneer, brother of a bishop and known as Tommy the Twister. All these had somehow come together in the mysterious Irish way and were giving their whole attention to the matter in hand with the earnest dedicated nondenominational faces of Irishmen and -women digging out fox cubs. Michael thoroughly enjoyed every moment of it, and when at last the four little balls of red wool were safe in one bag and in another the vixen, her face a mask of hate with its mad honey-coloured eyes and bared needle-sharp teeth, he came away as contented as if he had been industriously and gainfully employed all the while. I'll do the old tree tomorrow, he promised: Atracta and Tomo had the morning ruined on him anyhow and if he was never to please himself but only to toil and moil like a navvy, why, he'd be an old man before his time and Dulcie might chuck him, to marry Hugh. Really and truly, he explained to his conscience, you might say he had gone to dig the cubs out for Dulcie's sake and not his own at all. By the time he had reached the house and was sitting down to the grisly luncheon Atracta had devised on a decrepit oil stove he was no longer merely at peace with himself but feeling actively virtuous.

Seven

❀

THAT night Michael dreamed of Atracta as he so often
did, and she came naturally to his mind the instant he
awoke. He lay there thinking that one of the cardinal
errors they had made with her was their gradual acquiescence in her ways. Once upon a time he would complain of the things she did and give strict orders for the
future. She would overwhelm him with snivelling excuses
and tedious assurances of humility, after which all went
on as before. Nowadays, although he still reviled her, he
no longer really tried to bring about a change because
there was so much else to be thought of and because he
knew that under the pliant exterior was something ferociously intractable. The case of breakfast time was a
typical one. It was still theoretically at eight o'clock:
he had never countermanded the order for its being at

eight. Nevertheless he had, almost unconsciously, got in the habit of going for it about nine, of weakly accepting the fact that it would not be ready before. The routine of the house moved at Atracta's pace and on her level of human development.

He determined this morning to go down at eight sharp and raise Cain if breakfast were not ready, as a step towards convincing the wretch that his mind was made up. At seven-thirty he was out of bed and shaving, all eagerness for the fray. His hand was on the knob of his bedroom door as the hour began to strike. Then suddenly the great gong in the hall boomed out an imperious summons, as it had in days gone by. He stood there hardly able to believe his ears. No one ever sounded that gong now; it had become almost as much of a relic as the family portraits and the swords and medals in their glass-lidded cases. The habit of beating it at the open door to bring him in from the haggard to a meal, as conches were blown on plantations to call in the slaves, had been given up, Atracta having substituted for it her own voice, which carried a long way farther. His first thought was that one of the triplets was having a lark, in defiance of the rule which forbade them to pass the swing doors. No triplet, however, could produce that full, sustained peal of thunder, nor for that matter could Atracta herself. Yet there was nobody else in the building, except for his mother. He flung the door open just as Mrs Duff herself came out of her room in her old plaid, her hair down on her shoulders and an inquiring look on her face. As he hurried along the passage the gong fell silent and he heard light footsteps scamper towards the kitchen.

"I thought it must be you," he called to her.

"And I, that it was you," she replied. "How very tiresome of someone. Ballysimon had a trick of doing that, long ago. But he never called before breakfast." She retired again, saying "And Ballysimon is dead. If it is anyone else, I am not at home."

A still greater surprise awaited him in the hall. It had been thoroughly swept, the table, oak chest and cabinets polished; the glass shone and a log fire had been lit in the great fireplace. He could not remember when last he had seen it in this condition. Stunned, he went on to the dining room. Here too a fire burned merrily, a wood fire crackling and leaping in a clean grate instead of the usual lumps of damp turf smouldering on a bed of ashes. Breakfast was ready, the bacon and eggs piping hot, the tea and toast freshly made, the table neatly laid on a clean cloth.

For a moment he supposed that Atracta had been up and labouring since daybreak in a forlorn endeavour to regain his esteem and hold her place. But as he took the details in, it was evident that this could not have been her own unaided work. Here and there were traces of a culture entirely and forever alien. In the middle of the table, sitting primly on a mat, was a bowl of flowers, of different kinds and colours hideously clashing, but fresh picked and in clean water. The crusts had been taken off the toast, which had then been cut across to form triangles in a dainty, genteel manner. There was an indefinably urban and cosy air about the arrangements which it would have been quite beyond Atracta's power to bestow on them; but then, who could have done it?

Michael very much disliked anything in the shape of a mystery, anything but what was clear and open and plain for all to see. It was a reaction to the eternal, pointless secrecy in which the Gaels around him delighted. One of his main grievances against Atracta, indeed, was a certain element of the mysterious in her composition which teased at his mind so that he, a man by nature anything but introspective, continually thought of her, puzzled as to how a human being could behave as she did, and even wondered if she were really human at all. Any generalization he might chance to hear about the human race, and particularly one that was favourable to it, would set him off on one of these worried little meditations. A mystery like the present, then, on his very hearth, was more than he could tolerate and the moment he had finished breakfast he went to look into it.

He went down the passage and through the swing doors quickly and softly, as if burgling his own house, and paused outside the kitchen door to listen. What he expected to hear at this hour, if anything, was the squealing of the triplets and a furious banging and rattling as Atracta raked the ashes out of the stove. Now he distinctly heard the glad roar of a lighted fire and a man's tenor voice throatily singing a popular song in a strange accent. Very gently he opened the door an inch or two and listened again.

"Some dy me 'appy ahms'll 'old you . . ."

It appeared that Atracta had a follower, and one providentially well suited to her temperament, as he was engaged in sweeping the floor. Michael got a glimpse of the intruder from behind, a gnome of a man about five foot five inches, lean and bowlegged as a jockey, with thin red hair and the ears of a bat which, standing out like handles, gave the back of his head an oddly Mephistophelian air. There was a spruceness about the little fellow in his clean shoes and tidy suit that suggested him as the author of the refinements in the breakfast room. Michael pushed the door open and boldly went in.

"Good morning," he said.

The gnome swung round, with fear in his little sharp grey face. He looked like a foreign caricature of a cockney, with eyes close together and a mouth of big teeth square and yellow as if cut from orange peel. A damp cigarette end stuck to his lower lip. For a moment he stood there, palpitating like a startled rabbit, and then he slowly laid his broom aside and began taking off the flowered apron lent by Atracta.

"Rumbled already, eh?" he said philosophically, in a keen English voice, the cigarette stub wagging up and down as he spoke.

"Don't let me disturb you, please," Michael said. "Are you a friend of Atracta's?"

"Nah." The gnome hesitated, looking intently at Michael with little eyes full of the tired wisdom of great cities, assessing him, summing the chances up. " 'Usband," he shyly disclosed.

"Not Mr Alfred Smith!" In all the wedding photographs Michael had seen, the happy bridegroom had worn a top hat and, standing behind his seated bride, had appeared to be tall and of a commanding presence.

"The sime." A wary cunning came into the eyes. "She let on about me?"

"Never. We rather understood that you had parted."

Mr Smith emphatically shook his head and a look of deep tenderness passed over his features. "Nah. Never no parting. We was cruelly put asunder by man."

"I see." He did not see at all. "Where is Atracta now?" he inquired, for something to say.

The reply that Mr Smith made to this, made with all the simplicity of greatness, revealed that a grandiose new element was at work in the life of Georgetown. "Upstairs, governor. Miking your bed."

Michael deemed that he was joking. Atracta never made a bed before five in the evening and not infrequently had to be hunted up to do so at the moment its occupant wished to retire. If it came to that, she did not make the beds at all except on the day the sheets were changed, but contented herself with pulling the clothes straight and buffeting the pillows, burying pyjamas, nightdresses, handkerchiefs within as a dog buries his bones. But Mr Smith looked perfectly serious as he spoke.

"How did you get her to do it?" Atracta's employer asked with respect.

"How do I get 'er to do anything?" Mr Smith demanded rhetorically. He unbuttoned his jacket with a flourish and significantly tapped the belt round his waist. "A man's best friend," he said with a wink. "Oh, don't mistike me. We're the 'appiest couple on earth. As Woman I worship 'er. As Woman, she captivates me. I adore the Sex, but she's queen of them all. 'Other women cloy the appetites they feed, but she makes 'ungry where most she satisfies . . .' As Woman, mark you. As an 'uman being," Mr Smith said briskly as he buttoned his jacket again, "she calls for leather. It's the mentality."

Atracta bounced into the kitchen and dropped her brush and pan with a shriek. "I was going to tell you, Master Michael," she began whining. "Sure, didn't he come just yesterda' in the evening, and you with Herself at the telly . . ."

"Nark it," Mr Smith bade her, raising a bony hand; and the flow ceased, switched off at the main. "I understand," he proceeded weightily to Michael, "that there have been differences, governor. Words. Atmosphere. I believe you expressed a desire for change. Nark it," he said again to the queen of her sex, in case she contemplated utterance.

By now Michael was beginning to look on the new-comer with awe. He himself could never have silenced the woman in that calm and resolute way: conversations with her as a rule could only end by him dashing out of the room. His mind was fairly spinning, too, from the conception of Atracta as odalisque and *femme fatale* . . . "Well, yes, I suppose so," was all he found to say.

"The trouble," Mr Alfred Smith resumed, "was, lack of supervision. We see the sime all over the troubled world of today. We are 'oist with our own democratic petard. People are just not ready. It's the mentality. From now on there will be supervision." He made as if to unbutton his coat but changed his mind. "If then not satisfied you have only to sy so. And I, Mrs Alfred Smith and the nippers will pass out of your life, and on to the unknown."

"But do you want employment here?" Michael asked.

"Certainly not," Mr Smith replied, with a touch of hauteur. "I call no man master. A touch here, a touch there: no steady work. What I offer, I'm telling you, is supervision. And be'ind supervision, there's leather. Tike it or leave it, governor, but you could do worse."

"I'll speak to my mother," Michael said, thoroughly dazed. Atracta stood looking at him with contentment glowing in her yellow eyes, not joy, happiness or relief, but the mindless contentment of an animal coming in from the cold and wet to a fire. For his part, having had his say, Mr Smith was all impassive detachment, as if Michael's decision would hardly affect him one way or the other.

Mrs Duff was in the dining room staring in amazement at the sideboard. "Where did she find the chafing dishes, Michael?" she asked. "They have been missing for years."

"Atracta's husband did it. He is here and," Michael said simply, "I think he may be a genius."

"Atracta's husband? How very extraordinary." Mrs Duff ruminated a little. "There will be more triplets," she announced.

"He wants to stay here and keep Atracta in order. Mother, he's positively uncanny!"

As if to bear this statement out, Atracta came into the room at that moment, quietly and respectfully, with the morning's post on a salver. Her normal procedure was to throw it down on the scullery table, where it remained until one of them thought to fetch it. "Madam," she said to Mrs Duff, offering the side where two long brown envelopes with a harp on them lay. "Master Michael, sir," she said, politely wheeling the salver so that he could take his daily quota of bills, reminders and threats. As she left the room they nerved themselves for the customary slam of the door: she closed it behind her as suavely as a Hollywood butler.

"The man had better stay," said Mrs Duff. But in the next moment Mr Smith was forgotten. "Oh! It's more Molly," she exclaimed, shattered and desperate, her voice rising. "Why are they plaguing me, Michael? Can't you stop them, darling boy? What can they want?"

He soothed her, taking the letters out of her hand and promising to call on Father Behan the minute he had given the men their orders. With breakfast so wonderfully early he could well spare the time for this, and he found pleasure as well in the thought of seeing the priest again. He went out by the front door to avoid disturbing the happy pair in the kitchen but Atracta was there before him, kneeling, scrubbing the grimy stone steps as if her life depended on it, while Smith looked benignly on with folded arms.

"All right, Smith!" Michael called out without stopping as he went to the haggard. "We'll try it out."

The little man came pattering after him and laid an arm on his sleeve. "*Mister* Smith, governor, if you've no objection," he whispered conspiratorially. "As long as she's present, that is. Prestige, and all that kind of lark. It's the mentality."

Michael wished to hear more, much more, of the Smith school of imperialism, its theory and practice, aims, philosophy and, if any, its limitations: he would have liked to know, too, if Mr Smith had as it were been born to the purple, or worked his way up to it. But he could not dally. Dano was as lame as ever and Paddy had not appeared today, as a mark of displeasure at having been made to cleanse the kitchen after the bull. Michael went his rounds in high spirits this morning, none the less. Smith had all but driven Atracta, Georgetown, debts and even Dulcie herself to the back of his mind.

Later on he found Father Behan at work in his garden, wearing a blue apron over his shabby cassock and looking almost happy. This habit of gardening, cooking, washing and cleaning for himself was an eccentricity of his that troubled his flock more than any other. To begin with, a housekeeper was essential to the smooth running of the village grapevine; and then they were shamed before the surrounding parishes. All these had fine stout priests in good suits and with many chins, who lived in a style befitting their rank and redounding to their people's credit, while Father Behan was as thin as a rake and went everywhere on a rattling rusting bicycle. He took nothing from the parish fund but for the bare necessities of life, thus depriving the faithful of their birthright pleasure of grumbling at him. It was openly said, moreover, that this wild scarecrow was all the people of Crummagh could afford, which stung them to the quick, particularly as in the high days of Father Murphy they had been the admiration of the county.

Having greeted his visitor in the matter-of-fact way he had used at their first encounter, Father Behan took the two letters that had so tormented Mrs Duff, read them through and gave a short dry laugh. "Isn't it well for them that have nothing to do?" he remarked. "These are about the same matter as before. One says, will you reply to the earlier communication at once, failing which the parcel will be returned to sender. The other, from a different office, says will you go there and collect it yourself, when the straw will be destroyed in your presence."

"All the way to Dublin! I daresay. And nothing about what's in it, or where it came from?"

"Not at all. I suppose now," Father Behan said, fixing Michael with understanding, melancholy eyes that were clear and brown as a stream in the hill, "that these communications upset your mother."

"They do—how did you know?" Michael asked, surprised. Father Behan made no reply, merely saying as he had done before, "Thank you for coming, child," and turning away to his work.

The young man was on the point of accepting this dismissal when his eye happened to fall on what Father Behan was at present doing. The whole square plot of ground, in Father Murphy's time so gay with lobelia and geranium and aster, was a riot of gnarled yellow cabbage and Brussels-sprout stalks, thin raspberry canes, sour green rhubarb and rampant couch grass. It was not without a certain bleak grandeur, as if Father Behan's unquiet soul were expressed there in vegetation. He was busy now putting down seed potatoes, stabbing the earth with a pointed stake to a depth of six or seven inches where, like Truth in her well, the tuber was to lie *perdu*. He *is* mad, after all, Michael thought. No man in his right mind ever set potatoes like that.

"Excuse me, Father, but those drills are very deep," he observed with diffidence.

These few words had a strange, powerful effect on the holy man. He straightened up with a jerk, swept a long grey lock of hair from his eyes and looked at Michael in a combative way. "They are no such a thing, then!" he retorted.

"Excuse me, Father, they are," Michael persisted. He could not bear any trifling with potatoes. "And that isn't the place for them—they'll collect all the damp of the garden. And they ought to have been in long ago."

Father Behan was suddenly in a towering rage. "Will you hark at him, now! Will you!" he cried. "I grew potatoes before you were born, you . . . you sparrow! And I was reared in Ballydolan where they know what potatoes are. There is not a potato fit for a Christian this side the Blackwater. And me little lad ups and tells ME how to set potatoes. Too deep! says he. Too damp! says he. And too late! says he." Father Behan fiercely mimicked the Anglo-Irish accent. "Sure, I never heard such damned bloody impudence in all of me life before!" He crossed his two great work-swollen hands on the top of the stake and leaned on them, breathing hard and scowling.

"And I never saw such damned bloody incompetence in all my life before," Michael rejoined with spirit. "And never mind the accent, Father Behan. The reason I don't talk like a bog man is just that I'm not one."

"Is that how you address a man of the cloth?"

"Bother your cloth!"

Rearing himself to his great height, Father Behan

widely opened his mouth in order to pronounce a com-
mination that would pierce the culprit like a shaft from
Heaven and blast him entirely out of the garden. Even as
he did so, however, a sudden awesome change came over
his demeanour. All at once he was racked by inward
struggle, by spiritual conflict so cruel that he shivered
and gasped like a man in a fit. "Will you never have
done?" burst through his clenched teeth in a voice of
agony. Then just as suddenly again he was limp and
spent, with drops of moisture gathering on his brow:
and for the first time Michael saw him smile, a slow
sweet rueful smile that entirely changed his face.

"That was the Devil," he explained. "He's gone off
now. Child, I ask your forgiveness. It was a nice way to
talk, all right."

"Oh, Father, I'm the one to say that," Michael said.

"Pride, damnable pride!" the priest lamented. "It
could not bear the truth. For it was the truth, no doubt
of it. My potatoes rarely succeed and I've often wondered why."

"Wait a bit," Michael said, whipping his jacket off.
"Have you a spade anywhere?"

"I had, till Jimmy Hogan borrowed it."

"That one! Never give him the lend of a stick,"
Michael counselled. "But I'll manage." He worked
away in silence using the awkward stake as best he could
until all the tubers were planted in three good rows.
"They'll do if its not too wet," he said then, straighten-
ing his aching back. "But this clay is heavy on them. And

(105)

don't delay with earthing up, or they'll go sour on you."

"That was a kind thing, Michael," the priest said. He had been watching the young man's labour with close attention. "Is all well at home?"

"I should think it is, Father!" Michael said with a laugh, putting his jacket on. "Atracta's husband has bobbed up from nowhere, and he's able for her!"

"You don't mean it!" Father Behan exclaimed, looking at him intently. It was clear that he knew much more about the Smith family and their complicated situation than their employer could hope to do. Next he began putting questions, as to when exactly Smith had come and from where, what kind of a man he was, what account of himself he had given and what his intentions appeared to be, which Michael answered where he could, half amused and half irritated by the priest's assumption of authority.

"You will tell Mrs Smith I wish to see her," Father Behan directed, when his interrogation was done. Then his manner changed once more, in the way that seemed habitual with it. "God bless you, child," he said. "I'll not forget the potatoes. There's nothing in the house or I'd ask you in. My respects to your mother and tell her, don't mind the fellows in Dublin. Sure, they're only pretending to earn their pay." And again there was the bewildering shift of temper. "I shouldn't have said that!" he moaned, wringing his enormous hands. "Oh, I'm a fine one!" He rushed into the house without another word and could be heard addressing complaints to a presence inside.

Michael drove off, marvelling. Was Father Behan mad or was he not? Sometimes he was sanity itself, at others . . . It might be simply the effect of a country parish in Ireland after the order and peace of a Liverpool slum. It occurred to him, too, that the priest had come to Crummagh just when the McCloskey scandal was at its height. McCloskey had been an official in the Department of Health, one of whose duties was to endorse the doctors' recommendations concerning the detention of lunatics in state asylums; and who, from pressure of work, malice or misguided humanity had countermanded them all instead. Lunatics by the hundred had been thrown on the country and swiftly and painlessly absorbed into the national life. Could Father Behan be one of those? Surely the Roman Bishop would not have countenanced anything of that kind? But there were those alarming rumours about the Bishop himself.

Presently his thoughts wandered off these impenetrable mysteries and turned instead to Smith, Smith the dazzler, the administrative, pragmatic and unambiguous, the answer to his prayers and the man for his money. He hurried homeward, with pleasant anticipation in his heart for once, rather than dull foreboding.

Eight

Now Mr Browning went, or as he put it himself was called, to an international study conference on Wittgenstein that UNESCO had organized at Uppsala. He declared it to be a terrible nuisance as well as a grievous interruption to his work; but, as always, he recognized and met the obligations laid upon him by intellectual eminence. For a week or so before he got off Rougemain was an inferno. Much of the time he was storming because clothes, studs, suitcases and keys could not be found, had indeed, as he suspected, hidden themselves. "The house is bewitched!" he would cry. When not so engaged he would go tirelessly through the paper he had composed, a matter of twelve hundred words, making tiny changes here and there and reading the whole thing over to Dulcie after each.

"Detail, detail." He smiled over the breakfast table one morning. "Baudelaire wrote sixty letters to his publisher about the commas in a single poem."

"Did he get paid for it, Papa?" his younger daughter wished to know.

She was ignored. The philosopher impressed on the two girls that his desk was not to be touched or his files looked at in his absence. Bridget was not even to enter the room and any cleaning or dusting was to be carried out by Dulcie herself. The catastrophe of the manuscript of Carlyle's *French Revolution* was to be borne in mind. He exhorted them both to frugality, laid an embargo on all entertainment and wrote out a list of involved instructions about his post.

At last he was gone.

Mrs Duff went to stay with a connection of hers in Mayo—she would nowadays only stay with relations, connections or people she had known for "ages." The recent attempt on her life left no room for doubt in her mind that something particularly fiendish was afoot, and Michael saw that a change of scene was imperative. With her went Bob the sheep dog, without whom she could not close an eye at night and to whom alone of created beings she talked coherently and at length. Michael drove them to the station, settled them both in the luggage van as Mrs Duff declined to leave Bob there alone, kissed the one, patted the other, tipped the guard and returned home feeling gay and light of heart.

"Isn't it wonderful?"

"Isn't it marvellous?"

"If it were always thus! What shall we do this afternoon?"

"Let us go for a drive in the trap."

He laughed and promised to come over early. This morning the very house felt calm and relaxed as if a pack of invisible demons had travelled northward with their mistress. A deep delicious silence reigned over all, due as much to the miracle worker Smith as to Mrs Duff's departure. One of Atracta's habits had always been to stand at the scullery door and scream remarks at the men in the haggard at the top of her lungs. She kept it up unflagging for half an hour at a time, was indeed obliged to do so if the conversation were to continue, as the men never answered. With the coming of Smith the practice had ended, and much else as well: her frightful singing, for example, her tea parties, her rosary chanting and the way she had of spreading her own and the triplets' personal laundry over the bushes in the garden to dry.

Michael could not think of Smith without feelings akin to love. There was little contact between them. The political discussions that Michael had so much looked forward to never took place. Sometimes he would catch a brief glimpse of the red head and bat-like ears as they whisked round a corner, heard the light steps in a passage or the sharp cool voice uttering words of command, but that was all. This man who in so short a time had transformed the household had no mind to push himself forward, preferring the realities of power to the acclaim of the multitude. Yet where that power was concerned he stopped at nothing. Walking by their cottage late one night Michael heard the hiss and whine of a leather belt and the gasps, moans, entreaties and humble assurances of its victim. He stood rooted to the ground telling himself that if he had a spark of manhood he would intervene. But apparently he had none: the moments ticked by and still he stood, entranced, and did nothing. At last the dreadful sounds came to an end and he heard Smith say with entire good humour, and not so much as out of breath, "There, my Queen, that will learn you to contradict"—simple words and few, with a double suggestion of imperial grandeur and limited monarchy that fairly took Michael's breath away.

When next he saw his bondwoman he looked at her with peculiar attention and noted that never had she appeared more serene and satisfied, more aglow with health and contentment.

The taming and harnessing of Atracta had affected his whole existence, so that Georgetown itself mysteriously became less of a burden. He marvelled to think that one mindless human being could have weighed so heavy, he much admired himself for having borne it all so long. With the departure of Mrs Duff the feeling of liberation overpowered him quite and he became as merry and foolish as a boy playing truant. He rushed over to Rougemain the instant luncheon was done, although at three o'clock he was to have seen a Mr Nolan about some grazing. He stayed with Dulcie until eleven at night, although he had faithfully promised his accountant to sit at home and attend to his income-tax return. Such matters he saw as frittering away his precious time, the real and earnest object of his life being to talk to Dulcie, kiss her and hold her hand.

All now was delightful to them both, even the letters of Mr Browning. The first of these, which began, "My dear Dulcinea, I know you are impatient to hear what I think of Sweden," made them laugh until they cried. They went to the Hunt Gymkhana and Michael jumped Dano in two of the competitions, being placed third and then second. Dulcie declared these results to be a disgrace, alleging that the chief winners were all relations of the judges and had been lavishly entertaining them for some while back, and that the judges themselves, if it came to that, could hardly tell one end of a horse from the other; and that everyone knew these country shows in Ireland were as crooked as could be. Dulcie herself had entered The Walnut and her trap in a contest for the smartest one-pony turnout. She was so fond of the little vehicle and so proud of The Walnut that she was blind to trifles such as two loose wheels, a broken shaft, reins mended with twine and paint peeling off in long strips. She took her place among the showy equipages and high-stepping animals with a beautiful confidence and, blithely unaware of the onlookers' smiles, drove briskly round and round the ring, her wheels crazily a-wobble and a cloud of oats blowing up from the floor where a sack had spilled. Michael, weak with laughter, looked on and adored her.

He rang up the next morning and said, "Did you forget it was the Hunt Ball tonight? What shall you wear?"

"Oh, Michael! I told you I had nothing. My yellow satin."

"That old thing? Fi!"

"Then I'll have to take the sleeves out of the chiffon with the blue roses and add them onto the length."

"A repulsive suggestion. Woman," said Michael gravely, "the day we got engaged you undertook to commission a dress suited to your new importance from Mrs Twomey."

Mrs Twomey was the local dressmaker, an indifferent needlewoman but a British Army Widow.

"And so I did," Dulcie replied. "But that was only two years ago. Mrs Twomey never makes under three, as you well know, and with a long skirt it may be four."

"You'll be too old to dance by the time you get it. For heaven's sake don't let her make your wedding dress, or we shan't be able to have any children."

"Don't, Michael, don't," she implored him.

There was a buzz, a squeak and a crackle and Mr Foley's voice came booming down the line: "Will the Christian ethos survive?"

"No," Michael replied without hesitation. "Good day."

Dulcie broke into silvery chuckles.

"Who's that at all?" Mr Foley inquired in a frosty tone, as he had been most enjoyably haranguing the chemist and was only now getting into his stride.

"The state hangman."

"Well now, Mr Duff, I'm surprised, I reely am."

"Would you mind getting off the line?" Michael coaxed him. "I require it urgently, for hanging someone." He was feeling light in the head for very bliss. Dulcie was gurgling away like a little brook. Mr Foley opined that when all was said and done civility cost a man nothing. There was more buzz and crackle and then the line was cut and all Michael's efforts to regain it were of no avail, as if subscribers were limited to a single throw of the dice. Tomo bicycled over to Rougemain with further details of the evening plan, a means of communication often resorted to when time was short.

The various houses large enough for a ball took it in turns to accommodate the Hunt, to save the expense of hiring rooms. The turns came round faster and faster as the ranks of the gentry thinned out. Ballysimon's place had fallen to the nuns and Major White's old Georgian house had recently been demolished by a German who bought it to make way for a red-brick creation rife with spires, turrets and cupolas. Major Buchanan had been exempted for life after a dancer had put his foot through a board in the ballroom and, although he danced vigorously on, claimed the following day that his leg and his nerves would never be the same again, that his wife, at present in an interesting condition, was suffering from shock, that he had missed an appointment and very likely a fortune on the morning after and that he had been told for certain (but would mention no names) that the floor had been declared unsafe five years before: it had cost the Major seven pounds thirteen and he had hardly spoken of anything else for the six months that came after it. Mr Browning would not allow Rougemain to be used at all, fearing an interruption to his work; and Captain Deller's house was eliminated as someone thought she had seen a ghost there, with prejudicial effect on the box office.

This year was the turn of Castle Kilrany. The master of it had displayed the confidence he had in his fellow men of whatever social degree by moving every single article of any value at all to an upper floor and barring ingress thereto by rolls of barbed wire. Men with guns were patrolling the gardens, greenhouses and park lands. Resplendent in scarlet tails, his lean blue jaws hard at work, Kilrany stood by the hall door and kept a sardonic eye on the guests as they arrived.

"Shabby little dress, that," he said to Dulcie, frowning at her yellow satin. He seized her and kissed her hard. "Buck up and marry Michael," he commanded. "Then you'll be a relation and I can do that often." Coming from Kilrany this was an exquisitely phrased compliment. "Bugger off," he continued to a little man in spectacles who was pressing anti-blood-sport leaflets on all who would take them. The little chap looked round in terror. "Yes, you, sir, you with the snotty nose." The little man trotted away into the night. "McCarthy!" Kilrany bawled. "If you see any more of those fellas, shoot 'em. And nail their hides to the gate."

"I will, of course," the gamekeeper responded from a lair in the shadows. "I don't know at all how that one got through."

"Upon my soul! Anti-this, anti-that. What's Ireland coming to?"

Now the dance band from Cork began to play and Michael hurried Dulcie into the ballroom. It was a vast dim place with a dusty unlit chandelier in the centre and clean patches on the walls where the pictures had all been taken away. Beside the door was a tray of French chalk in which the dancers were ordered to dip their shoes: Kilrany had come on this dodge described in a tale by Somerville and Ross and seeing nothing funny in it had adopted it at once, as a cheap and practical method of polishing the floor. A flock of country girls in clouds of tulle were huddled in a corner like sheep in the rain, throwing glances of despair at the conservatory at the farther end where their swains were fighting like wasps around the bar. Some of the Hunt members were dancing together, in a florid nineteenth-century style. Mr Goldfarb, a candidate for the Dail, tripped round the room with a kindly word for all, his oriental features set off in delightful fashion by his saffron kilt.

The two young people had the first four dances together and then Michael courteously partnered the

Master while Dulcie politely stood up with the Chairman. He was free at last from the plaster jacket which had so long delayed the holding of the Ball this year, but creaked in every joint and wheezed away like an old kettle. Their duty behind them, they were beginning the sixth dance together when Kilrany stalked up and took Dulcie to himself without a word. He danced well, although he held her in a grip of iron and maintained a severe silence throughout. Glancing up now and again at the dark chin above her head Dulcie thought that, yes, she was glad Kilrany would be a relation some day. Everyone and everything belonging to Michael had a glamour for her just now, even his potty old mother. Kilrany looked down at the fine little head with its silky yellow curls and tried to estimate the owner's weight: seven stone eight on the hoof, as he judged it. When the dance was over he led her away to a secret buffet established in the library for friends and Hunt members only, where Michael, with flushed face and sparkling eyes, was in the act of prising open a bottle of champagne.

"Michael, you're mad! The extravagence!"

He poured out a glass for her and one for Kilrany. "It's the first day of Friday!" he said, laughing. "Here's to Uppsala! Up Mayo! Coupled with the immortal and glorious name of Smith!" He leaned over and kissed her with keen enjoyment.

"No farmyard stuff, I beg," Kilrany admonished them. A moment later his grim expression eased as a cry of pain came from somewhere in the grounds, followed by confused appeals for help. "Might be the senator," he commented. "Shan't know till McCarthy lays out the bag at the end of the evening."

"I didn't hear the shot," Michael said. "You wouldn't stoop to setting snares, sure you wouldn't?"

"Bear pit," Kilrany replied. "Wheeze of McCarthy's. A very useful chap, McCarthy."

The Master came in and seized Kilrany by the cuff. "Are you not going to dance with me, pray, young Hugh?" she demanded. She was wearing a garment wrought by herself from an old velvet curtain, as she regarded all clothing not for wear in the field as a waste of money and effort.

"I suppose there's no help for it," Kilrany answered with a frown. He swallowed his champagne and bustled her off to the ballroom, where the band was now earnestly rendering the "Blue Danube." As they went along he emphasized that it would be the one dance, and then no more: let there be no mistake about it, please, and no argument.

"What a rude old thing he is," Dulcie remarked, looking after him with a smile.

"It's the bottled-up frenzy," Michael explained. He sighed, looking pensively at the little beads of air in the wine. "Would a girl find him attractive?" he inquired in a subtle masculine way, his tone carefully unconcerned.

"Not this girl, dear silly!"

"All very well, I must watch my interests," he

pointed out. "You're the only female I know of under fifty-eight within a radius of a hundred miles. Two hundred miles. Darling, let's go off, just the two of us, do let's!" he cried. "Damn dancing! Let's look at the television. Or no, that'll soon be over. Tell you what—we'll drive to Dreenagh Bay and dance by the light of the moon."

Dulcie was just in the mood for a forty-mile drive in the moonlight and a caper on the clean white sands of Dreenagh at dead of night; and practical as ever she at once drew up a plan. They were first to drink up all the champagne, to avoid a wicked waste; and then to get a safe conduct from Kilrany, to avoid being shot by his men. Then they would drive to Dreenagh via Rougemain, where they would pick up some cans of petrol, to avoid being stranded all night and having to return home in their evening clothes by daylight, under the hosts of censorious eyes that lurked behind the dingy lace curtains of Holy Ireland. Rejoicing in the mental powers of his beloved, Michael agreed to all and gaily started to pour the wine; but just then Major Buchanan put his worried old face round the door.

"Michael, you're wanted," he said. "The Chairman's down. In the ballroom. No business at all to be waltzing."

Nowadays there were melancholy incidents at nearly every Hunt Ball, tumbles, seizures, strokes . . .

"Coming," poor Michael responded. Oh, it would, he would, they would: the entire universe was leagued together in the firm resolve never to allow him to have Dulcie to himself for a single hour, of that he was perfectly sure.

The old Chairman lay on the ballroom floor, his head supported by Kilrany's arm, breathing stertorously. With his craggy profile, closed eyes and clasped hands he looked like the figure on a Crusader's tomb. At Kilrany's order the band had continued to play, but no one was dancing. The social elements had separated like oil and water, one cool, collected and helpful, the other crowding together and excitedly murmuring as they snuffed disaster.

"Afraid I'm going to kick the bucket," the Chairman muttered apologetically. A dreadful sadness came into his face, for he had always hoped to go with the sweet cry of hounds in his ears and the "Blue Danube" was but a wretched makeshift.

"Yes, do, by all means," Kilrany replied, loosening the patient's collar. "Then I can stop the ball."

"Selfish young swine," the Chairman remarked, chuckling.

"Hush, don't talk. My dear man, you'll bury *me*, no fear of that." Kilranys never died in their beds and few of them saw fifty. "Eulalia!" Kilrany called to the Master of Foxhounds and nothing brought the gravity of the case more poignantly home to his hearers than this mode of address—"Eulalia, there must be a leech or two in all this rabble. Could you round one up and bring it here?

Michael, a glass of water, then tell McCarthy to bring a gate and a man."

They hurried off on their errands. With memories of the *Titanic* stirring under his thatch of hair the band leader came up to ask Kilrany if he should play "Abide with Me," to be rewarded with a glance of such concentrated loathing as sent him reeling back in disorder. The Master returned with the news that the only leeches present were an English lady doctor from Sevenoaks, on holiday in the area and the guest tonight of the Mayor of Ballinaduff, and a medical student from Galway. On hearing these facts the Chairman begged to be shot. Michael came with the men and the gate, and the four young men carried the old one carefully upstairs and settled him in a bed that, with habitual disillusion, Kilrany had caused to be made up with the other festive preparations. He sat beside it himself with a hand on the Chairman's shoulder while Michael went in search of an acceptable leech and the band, far off, fervently played "D'ye Ken John Peel" in the belief that it was a Protestant hymn.

The local doctor, dragged from his bridge, arrived presently and said that there was no immediate danger but the patient could not be moved for at least a fortnight. Kilrany observed that it was just his filthy luck. The doctor added that the patient's dancing days were positively done, and Kilrany wished loudly to God he could say the same of his own. As he came stamping downstairs with a face of thunder after the interview, the senator's wife sidled archly up to him with a murmured request.

"Powder room, powder room?" he snarled. "I suppose you mean a w.c. My good creature, this is not a railway station."

All were delighted to see Kilrany himself again.

"May I take Dulcie away?" Michael pleaded, as soon as he decently might.

"Do. Keep to the main avenue going out, and you'll come to no harm. There are notices up, to say where is safe," said Kilrany, a hard man but just. "McCarthy," he called to the darkness, looking a little more cheerful. "You may start the drive of the courting couples. Don't fire till you see the whites of their eyes."

"Right-o," McCarthy's voice came back.

Kilrany marched back to the ballroom, where he informed the assembly that he was sorry for their disappointment but all was well and they could put their rosaries up; and notified the band that if they didn't stop arsing about pretty soon they shouldn't collect a penny piece of their fee. With that he retired to the private bar and was not seen again that night.

"Ah, he's a lovely gentleman, all the same!"

"Isn't he the spit of his father, God rest him? Language and all."

"The good old sort, mind you. The real old stock."

After a whispered consultation the band started to

play "Darling, I am Growing Older." All the local lads returned to the bar without further waste of time, and the girls began dancing together.

Michael drove at breakneck speed down the avenue until they were beyond the range of McCarthy and his janissaries. He chortled gently to himself from time to time and stole a glance at Dulcie's profile. Unless the car itself broke down, nothing, he supposed, could interfere with their programme, try as it might. But even as he slowed down at the gates and began turning into the road a small weary figure wheeling a bicycle stepped into the glare of his lights. Michael knew him at once: the face, hair and ears could only belong to one man and in the same moment the well-known English voice called to him while its owner peered anxiously through the windscreen.

"That you, governor? Been trying to get you on the phone for hours. Cor! Must have got every other blinking number in the blinking county."

"And what is it, Smith?" With death in his heart Michael divined that the universe was up to its tricks again.

"One of the nippers, gov. Benedict. Swallowed a corkscrew. Matter o' life and death. Stone the crows!" Smith cried, flinging his arms out and addressing the world as a whole. "Not a day goes by but one of 'em swallows something. Bloomin' cormorants!"

"Well, then, he will have to be operated on, won't

he?" Michael tried to speak patiently. "I'm sure the hospital will send an ambulance. You don't need me for that."

"But I do, gov, see? I do. It's the mentality. The old woman will 'ave it that surgery's a mortal sin and," Smith confessed, in perhaps some of the saddest words man ever spoke, "I can't do nothin' with her. Nothin'! Nothin'! Nothin'!"

Nine

THE establishment of the *pax smithiensis* had affected the triplets not less than it had their mother. Before it there had been a continous uproar as each of them struggled to focus her attention on himself, and the beastly noise they made was very delightful to her. She would sit by the hour, serene, fulfilled, in conditions that would have sent another mad. Soon after his coming, however, Smith had revived the doctrine that children were to be seen and not heard and, his words falling on stony ground, had expounded it with leather. Previously it had been their habit to bawl the house down at the first twinge of pain or discomfort: now Benedict sat and grunted in a corner of the kitchen until there was no overlooking the fact that something was gravely amiss.

Atracta was all for letting things be. "Sure, that old corkscrew was no good to anyone," she observed comfortably.

"Not much good to the nipper, and that's a fact," Smith retorted. "Now, my girl, look sharp and tell me where to find a doctor."

"Ah, what would we do with a doctor? Wouldn't it be a grand thing for the little one to be cured by God himself?" There was more than simple piety behind her words, for Smith had no money and she would have to pay for the visit, while God, on the other hand, would presumably do the job for nothing.

Smith as a canny imperial administrator had ever held aloof from religious belief or ritual of the subject; but he knew when to depart from normal policy. "Oh, come on, mate! What's the use of callin' on God when the boy's got a flippin' great corkscrew in his stummick? 'Ow's *God* going to get it out? Ben'll have to be opened up and the hobject extracted, and that's all about it."

It took a while for Atracta to seize the significance of what Smith had told her but when she did she revealed a spiritual force that her lord had not suspected and which defeated him. There was something immemorially splendid about the way in which, taking her stand on the new Pope's cyclamen, she refused to countenance or even contemplate surgery. Smith might, as he later confessed, equally well have talked to the wall.

"The nipper will croak, At," he threatened her.

"Sure, we all have to do that one day, Alf," she replied with a beatific smile. "Welcome the will of God!" She spoke a little absently, her brain already being occupied with plans for the funeral, wondering if she could get the loan of the car from Master Michael and of the black cloth coat—to the fur one she dared not aspire—from the mistress. When Paddy lost his ninth, Master Michael lent and drove the car and Paddy's Rita sat in it smiling and bowing to the populace like she was the Queen of England.

Smith, penniless and in a strange land, at grips with a power beyond reason and imagination, was in despair. Then he remembered that Michael was at the Hunt Ball and that, reading the invitation on the hall stand as he read any piece of paper his eye lit on, he had noted that the ball was to be at Castle Kilrany. There followed his vain endeavour to reach the castle by telephone and the lonely anxious ride in darkness on a decrepit bicycle, when he knocked on cottage doors to ask the way and time and again was misdirected.

It was a cruel blow to Michael to learn that Smith was not the absolute power that he had believed. He saw no hope whatever of himself succeeding where that redoubtable man had failed. None the less he immediately packed the bicycle on the roof of the car, installed Smith in the back, and drove home at top speed to make an attempt. Atracta was sitting by the hearth in her own cottage with Benedict on her lap, rocking him gently and looking down at him with the tenderness of a *mater dolorosa*. Benedict lay with closed eyes and flushed face, grunting like a sow in labour.

"Atracta, what is this? You must do as Smith tells you, you must," Michael began. "Don't you understand what will happen?"

"Welcome the will of God, Master Michael, honey," she replied bravely. "Though madam will be disappointed, missing the funeral and that."

"Cor stone the crows!" burst from the lips of Smith. "I seen everything!"

"But you are wrong, Atracta. You've got the wrong end of the stick about that encyclical. Father Behan told me so himself."

Atracta gave him an indulgent look, as one long versed in and immune to the devil's methods of subornation.

"Don't you want to save the child?" Dulcie asked, her eyes shining with anger.

"I want God to save him, Miss Dulcie, acushla."

"God helps those who help themselves."

Atracta let this naked avowal of Protestantism pass without comment and, secure on the rock of her faith, smiled on them all with the infuriating satisfaction of an early Christian martyr.

"You shall pay for the corkscrew, then!" Michael stormed, throwing in his last card. "I'll stop the amount from your wages!"

A threat of this kind would commonly reduce

Atracta to pulp but she never so much as blinked an eye. "God love you, Master Michael," she replied, " 'tis two months and more that you didn't pay me any wages at all. Ah, but I'd never blame you!"

"Oh, you halfwit." But abuse won't help matters much, he reasoned. Fuming, he dashed away in the car to get Father Behan, wondering even as he did so at the strange something that drove him on to save at all costs the life of Atracta's horrible offspring. It was after two when he got to the presbytery. A light shone in the downstairs room as it had done when first he had called there, but Father Behan was not haranguing the unseen presence tonight. He came to the door holding a candle and a sock he was mending and greeted Michael as if the small hours were a capital time for a visit. He quietly heard the story out, said "Come, there is no time to lose," and ran out to the motor car hatless and coatless.

He marched into the cottage without the least cere-mony, exclaiming, "You foolish woman! Stir yourself, the boy has to get to the hospital."

"Yes, Father," she agreed at once. "If you say so, Father." She made the volte-face without effort, emotion or embarrassment. Smith buried his face in his hands and groaned aloud.

"Have you a shawl or a blanket to wrap him?"

"I have, Father. Alf, would you ever get the shawl from me bed? I'll have him ready in a minute, Father."

The Smith who hurried out to get the shawl, in this way humbly acknowledging the fact of Father Behan's pre-eminence, was a Smith grey and limp and with the stuffing all knocked out. The whole way to the hospital, as Michael drove him and Benedict slowly and carefully along the rough roads, he was silent, ruminating with embittered perplexity on this new, amazing and dreadful side to his Cleopatra. Only when they got there and the house surgeon told him he should have brought the child in sooner did he display a touch of his former style.

"Not my fault, cock," he said sharply. "Religion and all that lark. It's the mentality."

"Stone the crows," he was heard to mutter wearily over and over again. He elected to remain at the hospital until the operation was over, as he did not trust the locals an inch: like as not, he told Michael, they'd amputate both the pore little perisher's legs by mistake. Michael left him there and drove back with the news. The presence in Atracta's cottage of the priest and Miss Browning of Rougemain at one and the same time, the delicious sense of importance that the whole affair of the corkscrew had given her, and the not too faraway prospect of being the central figure in a funeral had together worked up in her to an absolute fermentation of mind. She sat at the table and dispensed her appalling tea, her wicked bread and her shameful butter with a look on her face that was difficult for human beings to regard with composure. Father Behan on the other hand sat in front of the untasted refreshments with that terrible sadness so often to be seen in his eloquent features: Atracta had just been prattling to him of her hope that the triplets, if God willed she should rear them, might enter the priesthood.

In the days that followed Smith was completely restored to power. His word was law once again and leather was resorted to freely as the form of criticism he chose to employ. No trace of vainglory or the knowledge of her own ultimate, secret strength showed itself in Atracta's behaviour to him, which remained one of doglike submission. The matter had deeper, more lasting effects on Smith himself, who spared no pains by his meticulous supervision of her work and even by lending a hand himself to let Michael know he was once again in the saddle.

In this way the time passed happily for them all. Quite soon Benedict was home again, restored to his usual lamentably rude health. Michael worked hard and well and saw a great deal of Dulcie. They drove, rode, gardened and watched the television together. One evening there were pictures of another new African state celebrating its freedom, with a number of the newly emancipated happily throwing people they disapproved of out of topfloor windows. Dulcie did not at all care for this, but Michael thought you could not make an omelette without breaking eggs.

"Suppose we threw your father and my mother out of the window," he suggested. "Then we could get married at once."

"Now now now," Dulcie said, a little breathless, as she always was when he spoke about marriage.

When the blow fell, therefore, it was all the more bitter for being sudden and unexpected. Two men in plain clothes and one uniformed Guard called on Michael early in the morning and explained that they would have to take Smith away. His name was not Alfred Smith but Sidney Wheeler, and Atracta was not his wife but the last of three women with whom he had illegally gone through a form of marriage. For all that, Atracta was the love of his life. Apprehended, convicted and sentenced for the crime with her (the two previous offences being considered with it), he had run away from the prison-without-bars to which, with singular innocence, the authorities had relegated him. He had made immediate tracks for his Queen, and through a diabolical mischance was seen boarding the Irish Mail by the very constable who had first arrested him. Consigned to Wormwood Scrubs, his sentence woefully increased, he had again broken out, displaying a degree of pluck, energy and resource that made his colleagues proud to be criminal. Now, however, the authorities knew whither his ardent heart would lead him and a watch was kept on any station or port through which he might conceivably pass. He was picked up again, again penalized; and again he broke out, this time safely reaching Ireland disguised as a Girl Piper. There he had lain doggo, the balm of Atracta, the joy and liberation of Michael, while the authorities worked feverishly to discover her whereabouts.

"It was all over the papers, sir, with his picture," a detective said, eyeing Mr Duff with the fertile suspicion of his trade. "Do you not read them?"

"Good heavens, no," Michael answered, surprised. "Should I?"

The man sniffed. "Perhaps you would take us to the accused."

Smith bore his reverse in the high Roman fashion that was to be expected. When the little party arrived and deployed itself with practised movements to doors and windows, he was seated on the kitchen table eating an apple and watching Atracta peel potatoes. He sat unmoved while the arrest of Sidney Wheeler alias Antony Jones alias Antony Roberts alias Alfred Smith was read out, merely clicking his tongue in disgust when the recital was over.

"That's not the wy, mate," he grumbled. "You should 'ave cautioned me, see? You should 'ave drawn my attention to the fact I was not obliged to sy anything but anything I did sy would be taken down and might be used in evidence. Irish! Oh, 'ow I do 'ate slovenly procedure!" he exclaimed with sudden passion. "We see it all over the world tody. Everything done in this tinpot wy. Everyw'ere the sime pitiful old story. Premature independence!" Slowly he got off the table and put on his jacket, at the same time feasting his sharp little eyes on Atracta. "Goodbye, my Queen," he said with controlled emotion. "Just you mind wot I bin tellin' you, or you'll smart for it. 'O! w'ither 'ast thou led me, Egypt? See, 'ow I convey my shime out of thine eyes by looking back on wot I left be'ind stroy'd in dishonour . . .'"

"Let's go," a detective said.

" 'Let 'im that loves me strike me dead!' " Smith declaimed, lifting one impressive hand in the air. He seemed disposed to continue and then to change his mind, for he meekly allowed the gyves to be fastened on and walked away between his captors without a backward glance.

Atracta had been looking on meanwhile with her mouth open. She had heard all that was said and observed all that took place but was unable to piece the facts together in a coherent mental picture. Accordingly she applied for information to Michael, who stood by rooted to the ground in dejection, and let out one of her piercing howls as he explained their meaning. In the next moment, however, she cheered up again and pointed with a happy smile to the apple that Smith had been eating.

"Ah, he's coming back all the same," she chirped. "He'll be back in a minyoot. He was only codding. Sure, he'd never walk out, and the apple just begun. That's not his way at all."

"You may be right, Atracta. I'm sure I hope so," Michael said, as with slow, heavy steps and bowed head he made for the door.

Ten

Mrs Duff wrote to say that she was cutting her visit short. She gave no reason for this, fearing the letter might be seized, but the stress and disorder of her mind revealed themselves in the script, with dots and dashes and whirls wildly tumbling along one after the other. When she had sealed the evelope down she wrote on the back of it, as an afterthought: "Tell absolutely *no one* that I am coming back until I am there."

It was all on account of old Bob, the English sheep dog. Mrs Duff's connection, Miss Horneyold, lived in a dreaming crumbling old house half-smothered in trees and shrubs on the sheltered side of a promontory. Dotted over the purple-brown mountainside across the bay were neat white cabins, reflected in the sea at dawn and dusk as pillars of light: a chapel stood on the shore, and further up was the old cemetery, a tangle of briars and nettles with reeling celtic crosses on which local surnames appeared over and over again. At this time of year the wild rhododendrons were in bloom and the earth looked as if it were covered by patches of lilac cloud. It was a country of magic air and sparkling water, and of a calm loveliness that made anything untoward seem all the more sinister.

At first all went better than anyone could have expected. Mrs Duff went for solitary walks with Bob or pottered vaguely in the garden, enjoying the cold deep silence after the hurly-burly of Georgetown. Indoors, Miss Horneyold was a woman of few words and the one old servant she employed of even fewer. Outside, all that could be heard was the cry of gulls or the song of larks, the bleating of sheep or the barking of their guardian dogs. Then one after the other the ominous things began to happen, things simple in themselves and only understood when the terrifying climax was reached.

One evening after dinner the usually quiet and well-conducted Bob suddenly clawed at his muzzle and dragged it along the ground with foam dripping from his jaws. Some hard object was lodged deep in his throat, which it was beyond the power of either lady to remove. Miss Horneyold rang up Mr Clancy the vet. who lived nine miles away, but Mr Clancy was waiting for a mare to foal and could not come. There was nothing for it but to put Bob frothing and moaning into the back of the car and drive to Mr Clancy themselves. Clancy whipped the object out and unhesitatingly identified it as the bone of a mutton chop.

"Highly dangerous. One splinter in the bowel . . ." Brevity was a feature of the local conversation.

There seemed nothing very remarkable in that. Bob had never got a bone in his throat before but, on the other hand, there undoubtedly had been mutton chops for dinner. They decided to warn The Kitchen, as Rita Lavelle was called, against giving him any but large beef bones and they drove home again telling each other it might have been so much worse. But Mrs Duff was on one of her lonely walks the next morning when a countryman stepped from some bushes a little way ahead and stood waiting for her.

"Good day to you, ma'am," he said, politely lifting his cap, "what class of a dog is that one at all?"

"We call them Old English Sheep Dogs," Mrs Duff replied, although she did not deem it his place to inquire.

"You were driving him to Clancy's," the man went on ruminatively.

"Yes, poor old chap."

"In the nighttime, mind you," the man said then, stealing a crafty glance at her. "And in the spillin' rain and all."

"But what lovely weather today!" Mrs Duff remarked in a cool tone, and she turned back the way she had come, thinking that the people of Mayo were somewhat above themselves.

She did not begin to feel apprehensive until a few days later, when Bob got a thorn deep in his paw. Again, on the face of it this was nothing wonderful. Bob had got thorns right in there between the pads on four previous occasions. The first time he was still very young and she carried him, fat and woolly as an eight-month lamb, the two and a half miles to Georgetown one sweltering August day. The second time dear Captain Fothergill was walking with her and he gave Bob brandy before taking the thorn out by a complex and time-consuming method he had picked up in the African bush. They had spoken of it all through dinner that night. The third time she was alone on a Scottish moor and Bob was nearly as big as she was. Somehow, heaven knew how, she had extracted the thorn with a hairpin while Bob alternately bared his teeth and licked her hand, and once it was out she had fainted clean away. After that they slept awhile in the heather side by side, on their backs, their mouths open, exhausted. The fourth time they were blackberrying on the Georgetown lands and Michael was there and everything was all right. She had determined then to make little chamois boots for Bob while the blackberry season lasted, but for this or that reason never carried out her resolve.

But this was the fifth time and five was the most unlucky number for her. It affected her as the ace of spades or a broken mirror might affect others, and the fact that she could not remember, or had never known, why, only made it the more frightening. As they drove

Bob out to clever little Mr Clancy again she found herself trembling all over. They were hardly at home again when something occurred to bear out her worst forebodings. A uniformed Guard appeared to say, nicely and apologetically, that a man was complaining of a bite from a dog the size of two sheep and that Bob was required in the barracks above for a questioning. Mrs Duff uttered a faint shriek.

"Nonsense, Brian," Miss Horneyold said.

"There's five witnesses, miss," said the Guard lugubriously. "Waitin' for to identify him."

"Five!" moaned Mrs Duff.

"There'll be five hundred by tomorrow, I'm sure," Miss Horneyold returned, and a small grin flickered in Brian's face. "But the dog has never left our sight. And he's old and sleepy and he'd scarcely bite butter. So tell your witnesses go blackmail somebody else."

"They do be mountainy men, Miss Horneyold," pleaded the Guard. "And mountainy men are shockin' tenacious."

"So am I," she pointed out, and groaning in confirmation the Guard withdrew.

"Why do they allow such people to dress up like decent men?" Mrs Duff asked in tremulous tones. "Can the Castle do nothing to stop it?"

She was off now, drifting along on the current of her distress, on and away to the open sea. By leaving Georgetown, she realized too late, she had flown towards the peril and not away from it. Fate had arranged a terrible appointment with her here in Co. Mayo. The gentle hooting of the brown owl in the tree by her window all night long, the monotonous cry of the cuckoo all day, were both signals between the mountainy men, or from a mountainy man to The Kitchen. For whom could one trust?

"They looked so kind," she remarked to her hostess that evening. "They all came out of the trees and clustered round. They looked so friendly. I thought they were congratulating him, perhaps; he'd just got the M.C., it was in the paper that same morning. Then there was a bang and they all ran away, and he was lying there on the ground."

"Buck up, old dear," Miss Horneyold said gruffly.

Many times that night Mrs Duff got up from her bed and flitted about the house, making sure the doors were locked and the windows secure. Despite these precautions, at breakfast time Bob was gone, vanished without trace as if he never had been there. Mrs Duff collapsed and was laid on a sofa in the library. "He was all I had for my own," she whispered, and lay back with her eyes shut.

With Miss Horneyold action took precedence of thought, although she was strong in both. Armed only with a hunting crop, serenely confident that she and it together must be a match for all the mountainy boyos in Ireland, accompanied only by her fox terrier who screamed with excitement, she carried out a reconnaissance of the grounds. A number of small black cattle illicitly grazed at the upper end; by the waterfall two mild-eyed English trespassers were munching their lettuce sandwiches; a bedraggled eiderdown, missing from the Violet Room this year and more, hung limply from the boughs of a tree like a flag taken from the enemy. But there was no sign of Bob or his captors.

Miss Horneyold came back to the house and sat down in the drawing room to reflect, breathing hard through her short pugnacious nose. After a long and profound meditation she reached out a hand and pulled the bell. "Where is that dog, Rita?" she demanded, as The Kitchen wheezed and grumbled her way into the room.

"You could ask Dinny, Miss Pansy," The Kitchen said at once, showing no trace of surprise at the question.

"Dinny the Drunk, or Dinny the Hook?"

"Dinny the Drunk."

"And you couldn't say so before!"

"How'd I know I was needed? Sure, who else would it be?"

"Get him."

The Kitchen dragged herself away and returned in an hour to say she had Dinny the Drunk below, and bashtly drunk he was. By the time Miss Horneyold had finished work on him, however, he was as sober as he ever would be in this world again. The explanation of the affair was clear as the light of day, so clear that Miss Horneyold marvelled to think she had not seen it. Noting the care and affection lavished on Bob by his owner, the people concluded in their simple way that he must be worth a mint of money. Why else would she do it at all? They decided to borrow him for a bit and try could they breed by him from some of their own collie bitches. The local breed was lean, despondent and touchy, with dull eyes and spiky fur, and by crossing one or more of the bitches with the well-fed well-groomed self-assured Bob it was hoped to improve the strain. Nothing but the people's own innate delicacy and some little fear of being charged for the service had stopped them asking the owner's leave.

"If it is any consolation," Miss Horneyold said drily, "he is long past all that. He's long past nearly everything."

Dinny goggled at her, with his mouth open. "Then why does the lady be mourning him so?"

"As for you, you old blackguard, you ought to be horsewhipped. Or shot," Miss Horneyold informed him. "Horsewhipped *and* shot," she amended.

"Arrah, Miss Pansy dear, 'twas only a lind, not a shteal, and there's no harm done to a soul," Dinny remonstrated, his rheumy eyes giving him an unfounded air of penitence.

"Away out of this and fetch him to me."

Dinny went staggering up the mountain to the derelict shepherd's hut into which poor patient old Bob had been stuffed, while Miss Horneyold hastened to bring the good news to the owner.

"Whenever you're up against an impenetrable Irish

mystery," she remarked, "just think of the silliest and lowest solution you can. Then you'll be getting warm."

Alien common sense could no longer avail, however, because suddenly and quietly Mrs Duff had crossed the bar for good. Michael knew it the minute he saw her get slowly and wearily down from the train at Ballinaduff: how, he could not have told, for in all outward ways she was just as ever.

"That is the kind of thing those people always do," was her comment on Mr Smith's polygamy and gaol breaking.

That evening she came down to dinner in her wedding dress and the family diamonds with her fine, ravaged face carefully made up. After the meal she sat stroking Bob's head by the drawing-room fire which, since the removal of Mr Smith, had reverted to a smouldering heap of turf. Michael sat near her, not daring to open his mouth. Atracta came in with an apronful of damp fuel and stopped to look on, unaware of anything odd in the scene but smarting because the mistress had not said a single word to her either of greeting or sympathy since she came back.

"I declare to God, madam," she began in her fawning way, her yellow eyes full of resentment, "you think as much of that animal as of me, a Christian!"

Mrs Duff looked up at the woman in blank amazement. "As . . . as *much?*" And all at once she began to laugh. She went into peals of laughter that was not in the very least crazy or hysterical but clear and merry, she laughed as she had done when she was young, on and on and on. She leaned back in the chair to give herself up to it more completely, a slight little figure in the magnificent satin dress that was now a thought too large on her. Then suddenly, without warning, the note changed, she caught her breath, choked a little while and lay there quietly without moving. Virginia Duff had died laughing at Atracta.

Eleven

ALL that evening as Michael saw to things that had to
be seen to, and all that night as he lay in the great bed
and stared up at the black outline of the hangings, he
felt his mother near at hand, his mother as she had been
in his childhood, gay and beautiful, smelling nice and
wearing summery clothes. Not until the morning did he
realize that she was gone forever.

Bridget bicycled over from Rougemain first thing
with a letter from Mr Browning. It was a little masterpiece of tact and sympathy and understanding, as free
from trite or forced condolence as from implications
that all might conceivably be for the best; and he wrote
of Virginia Duff as the lovely brilliant creature she
once had been and, his words suggested, always would
be. Entrenched in the library, storming at the least inter-

ruption and even at one moment threatening to pack Anne Louise off to Canada, he had made draft upon draft until one of the perfect letters for which he was rightly noted took final shape. "I am lending you my Dulcie for as long as you need her," he concluded, "and Bridget will stay and help all she can as well. It is the one little thing I can do, my poor dear boy." Michael was deeply touched.

The men came early, did the minimal jobs in silence and went home as if it were Sunday. As a mark of respect and to throw an eye round, Mr Foley brought the letters himself, using the front door as befitted a state official. He wore a dark suit, and a black hat which he raised high in the air with solemn glee as Michael came towards him.

"God rest and forgive the dear lady," he declaimed with gusto. " 'Tis what we all must come to, Mr Duff . . ."

Michael gave him a stricken look and doubled like a hare on his tracks into the house. Among this morning's letters were two that finally brought his loss home to him. *Oh, darling, more Molly!* The words were uttered so plainly at his ear that he turned to face the speaker, and suddenly knew how alone he was.

He drove out to Father Behan at once with the Gaelic missives. Their contents did not signify now but he wanted to see the priest and hear him talk. The men on the road took off their caps instead of merely touching them, for of course every man jack of them had heard the news. This lovely morning it seemed to him the fields and woods and hills themselves were aware of what had happened and were radiant with malice. Father Behan was at his garden gate looking down the road from Georgetown as if expecting someone, and he led Michael into the shabby parlour without a word.

"I . . . I brought these," Michael stammered, sitting down on one of the chairs.

Father Behan sat down too and took the communications from him. "Off again," he said, glancing through them with a faint smile. "And they're in two minds about it, as before. That lad says, your mother's parcel has been returned to the sender. This one has it, the straw packing was destroyed and the contents forwarded to her, at her own risk. So now."

"What on earth can you do with chaps like that?" Michael asked. He forced himself to speak slowly and clearly, like one who is drunk and does not wish the fact to be known. "When all the old familiar excuses have been made, it is still outrageous."

He stopped and the pair were silent for a while. Father Behan was looking at him dreamily, as if his mind were far away.

"Did you know she was dead?" Now the words came tumbling out.

"I did," Father Behan said, simply. "When is the funeral to be?"

"Well—there are various relations in England and Scotland. I was telephoning half the night but I didn't get them all." Father Behan's nonchalance took Michael aback for he had expected something more, although he did not really know what.

"England is where you should go now, Michael."

"Ah, if I could!"

"You can." Father Behan stood up in the dismissive way he had. "Come talk to me after the funeral," he directed. "Two women of sense from my parish are on the way down to you at this minute, and they'll maybe find a means of quenching Mrs Smith."

The women of sense got to Georgetown ahead of the young master and moved calmly and easily about the house as if death were their province. When he came in the old house was slowly and painfully coming to life under their hands: they had thrown open doors and windows and now were cleaning and polishing, sweeping cobwebs from the walls, throwing away dead flowers, making beds for the family mourners, all at the behest of Father Behan, who had found time amidst his struggles with Satan to arrange it.

The women had not been able to quench Mrs Smith, however. It was at no time an easy matter and at the moment it would have been impossible. Atracta had pondered long and deeply the tragic event of the night before and had come to see it as the divine retribution in store for those who made light of Atracta. The mistress had been struck down in the very act of laughing at her. The grounds for her laughter were beyond her comprehension but the Almighty's stern rejoinder had given a tremendous fillip to her self-esteem. In her outward acts she was correct to the last detail: she howled like a factory siren on and off, she recited the rosary, hushed the triplets if they made a sound, poured out sententious clichés in a torrential flood and veiled her ginger curls in black: but her eyes glowed with an inward light and she moved with the bearing of those whom God has signally favoured.

Dulcie drove up, bringing a picnic lunch. Constraint fell on them both and at first they could not look at each other; but as they went across the hall a horrible din broke out in the drawing room and, startled, Dulcie caught Michael's hand.

Michael flung the drawing-room door open. "That will do, Atracta!" he shouted. "Didn't I say last night I wouldn't have it?"

Atracta was seated in Mrs Duff's chair and rocking wildly to and fro. "Wah oo wah oo wah oo wah!" she bawled, thinking the gentry, God help them, had no etiquette. "Wah oo wah oo wah oo wah!"

"Will you shut up?" Michael thundered. "Or will I break every bone in your body?"

"Me lovely mistress!" Atracta ululated. "Me sweet pretty dear that was all in all to me, and I to her!"

"Couldn't stand the sight of you."

"The wan that was a mother to me! The wan that never let me down! Wah oo wah oo wah oo wah!"

"She believes it all, I do declare," Dulcie remarked, fascinated.

"The wan that said if the Lord should take her I was to fall in for the mahogany chest of drawers and the little poor silver tray!" Atracta trumpeted, swivelling her blank eyes towards him. "Wah oo wah . . ."

"Pipe down, you Arab!" Michael was looking about him for something to throw.

"Sure, there's no need in the world to be shouting, Master Michael," Atracta reproved him, "and the dear dead lady upstairs." She left the room with the air of one who has fulfilled a duty, wagging her hips friskily from side to side.

"I'll swing for that woman! I'll swing for her yet!" her master panted.

"Not today, Michael. Do please be quiet."

"Sorry."

Kilrany walked in, his jaws working hard. " 'Lo, Dulcie. I'm fixing things up, Michael," he began, in his tone of suppressed fury. "Bilkin's brain has turned to blancmange. Don't be surprised if he treats us to the harvest festival sermon in error. What of the aunts?"

"Aunt Henrietta will come, if she may bring her poodle," Michael replied. "But Aunt Louisa will not, because cousin Nathaniel is coming and they do not speak. Nor will Aunts Angelica and Belle. I am sorry to say that Aunt Angelica is in gaol for contempt of court, arising out of a feud with her fishmonger; and Auntie Belle is back in the bin."

"Bless my soul," Kilrany said benignly. "Well well

well. We all have our little ways. And why will Aunt Louisa not speak to her only son? Small blame to her."

Michael hesitated, throwing a look of appeal at his betrothed while a faint colour crept into his face. "It seems that he has turned," he muttered.

"How d'ye mean, turned? Like meat?" Kilrany asked.

"You know what I mean, Hugh."

Kilrany's lean jaws ground to a standstill. "Not Roman, Michael?" he asked, in the gravest tone the others had ever heard him use. Michael hung his head and Dulcie gave a little gasp.

"*Wah oo wah oo wah oo wah!*" came floating down the stairs.

"Ugh!" Kilrany's jaws commenced their work again. "Surely, Michael, you won't have the fella here?"

"He's Family," Michael groaned. "And he's already on the way."

"Family, indeed!" Kilrany snapped. "I'm Family too. In fact, with most of us cooled, canned, certified or merely gaga, I might almost claim to be one of our policy makers. Can't prevent him coming to Aunt Virginia's funeral but I beg you, do stop short of having him in your house. Nice connection for Dulcie, what?" He stumped away.

"*Wah oo wah oo wah oo wah!*"

"Nathaniel, doing a thing like that!" Dulcie said, with wonder in her voice. "It never rains but it pours."

"Perhaps the world is coming to an end," Michael suggested; but he did not sound very hopeful.

Towards evening the relations began to trickle in. Miss Henrietta Grahame of Waterford was the first to arrive, with little baggage beyond the poodle, the poodle's basket and the poodle's boxes of patent food. She was followed by Miss Pansy Horneyold from Mayo, who had picked up and brought along her brother Colonel Horneyold from Co. Clare. He retired to bed at once with a twinge of gout: the two ladies gossiped in low tones by the drawing-room fire. After dinner came Miss Felicity Duff, who spoke French and played the piano, and who had to sleep on the top floor lest someone should climb in at a window and get her. Near midnight Great-uncle Evelyn rang up, very muddled, to say he was at Limerick station and would somebody fetch him: he had selflessly mismanaged the estate during Michael's minority and in consequence looked upon himself as a privileged person there. Morning brought the English contingent, Great-uncle Frederick Duff (R.N., retired), who wished, despite existing arrangements, to commit his niece's body to the deep, and cousin Nathaniel Waverley, who ostentatiously crossed himself before he ate, to the general dismay. The relations from Scotland were last and consisted of Virginia Duff's sister-in-law, poor Mary Grahame as she was always called, and Elizabeth Hamilton, a cousin who bred Airedales near Berwick-on-Tweed. None of these people had met each other for a long time.

"I always say, there's nothing like a funeral," Great-uncle Evelyn remarked with satisfaction. "Except of course the Dublin Horse Show."

"Deuced lot of bother getting here, that's the only thing," Great-uncle Frederick replied.

"Well, you'll be next, I imagine," Great-uncle Evelyn said. "Then we'll have to go over there."

The two old men laughed and laughed, digging each other's ribs.

Poor Mary Grahame was asked nowhere unless she had to be and to compensate herself had developed the art of being tiresome to an extravagant pitch. The diet she was obliged to follow could not, she declared, be interrupted without very grave risk to her health. It included such items as Bircher-Benner's *Muesli*, peanut butter, rye bread, celery salt, *tisane de tilleul* and sour milk, none of which, to her aggrieved surprise, was to be had at Georgetown. In normal times the supply of sour milk was plentiful all the year round because Atracta never washed the jugs, but now, what with prayer and lamentations and the lookout for souvenirs, she had yielded the kitchen and pantry up to the women of sense and Bridget of Rougemain. Poor Mary Grahame grizzled and whined and then, recollecting the sad occasion, put on a bright and forgiving smile.

It was from the beginning a restless unhappy little assembly. Old Bob ran from one person to the next looking piteously into their faces, as if they might be able to give him news of his mistress. Colonel Horneyold's gout grew steadily worse, as he had known it would. He had not wanted to come at all but Pansy insisted, pointing out that dear old Virginia went round the bend in her house and near as dammit conked out there. The Colonel sat all day in the library, muttering to himself with his leg on a stool and glowering if anyone opened the door. Miss Felicity Duff was in one of her difficult phases: her eyes glittered, her squealing laughter never died away and her long loose grey hair tumbled wildly down her back. "Why could not some poor fellow have married her?" the Family mused, as it had done these thirty years: a native solicitor, almost, might have been better than this. Miss Hamilton had left the keys of her luggage at home, which at once reminded poor Mary Grahame that she had done the same thing before, the time she had visited *her*; and Miss Henrietta Grahame was engrossed in the poodle, overexcited by his journey and yodelling the house down. Only the two old great-uncles maintained their fearful gaiety.

More provoking than all the rest together was cousin Nathaniel. "Where can I find a Catholic priest?" he demanded of Michael the instant breakfast was over on his second day. "I shall need a dispensation to attend the service."

"Oh, couldn't you have seen to it in London?"

"Better in the parish itself," Nathaniel explained importantly. "One should avoid causing scandal or upset."

"We don't count, of course," Michael said. "Anyway, who's to know?"

"Everybody will know," his cousin assured him. "They will see me at Mass on Sundays."

Michael could feel the gooseflesh prickling up and down his arms and legs. "On Sundays? Do you mean to stay, then?" The words came out as if torn from his lips.

"Well yes, I do. I'm taking my annual leave now in order to do so. I couldn't have come all this way for nothing," Nathaniel told him frankly. He was something to do with the BBC. "Mother won't have me at home and I can't afford to go away. And you mustn't be left alone to mope. It is really an ideal arrangement."

"The parish priest is said to be mad," Michael said to gain time, in a voice dulled with misery.

"That is the kind of thing Protestants always say," Nathaniel answered loftily.

"No, the people say it."

"That I find hard to believe," Nathaniel said in the same tone. "The loyalty of the simple Irish people to their clergy is proverbial."

"Oh, don't tell me about Ireland just now, there's a dear chap."

"Sorry." Nathaniel stalked away with his nose in the air. Presently he was back again, looking rather subdued. "He is rather strange, all right," he conceded. "I asked for the dispensation—it's a mere formality, you know—and he stared at me as if I had nothing on and then refused it. Refused it, knowing who I was!"

"So you won't be able to come," Michael said, loving Father Behan more than ever.

"Not come? Not come to Aunt Virginia's funeral? What next? Most certainly I shall come."

Atracta came swinging up with a parcel in her hands and the news that there was twelve and sixpence to pay. This, then, must be the long-awaited packet that gave rise to all the Molly: as he received it in his hands Michael thought how light, how little, it weighed against the upheaval it had caused, and as he emptied his pockets, borrowing four and eightpence from Nathaniel to make up the sum, he felt grief pour into his heart as if through a dyke that was holed. He carried the parcel off to the bailiff's den and shut the door behind him. Labels in Irish were stuck about the paper wrapping, lending an air of mystery and importance, and the string ends were tidily secured in an official metal seal. Someone had done his work thoroughly and conscientiously.

Michael opened the parcel and studied the contents, his lips tubed in a thoughtful whistle. He was staggered, and yet not in the least surprised. The Customs had apparently been in three minds about the affair rather than two, for they had sent on the straw packing and nothing else. No doubt the contents had been destroyed, to hinder the spread of foot-and-mouth. There was no letter within, no declaration without, the writing in the address was unknown and the postmark a blur.

Wow-oo wow-oo wow-oo! Urrrrr! came from the hallway. Michael drummed with his feet on the floor and called out through clenched teeth, "Will you stop that filthy row?"

The door opened and Miss Grahame appeared, rather pink-cheeked and bright-eyed. "We are sure we are very sorry, Michael," she began with stately composure. "This is a strange place for us. And we are still feeling the effects of our journey. We had to travel in our basket, in the luggage van with the Guard."

Wow-ah-oo! the poodle mournfully chimed in.

"I do beg your pardon, Aunt Henrietta. I assumed that it was Atracta." He saw that she was looking at him attentively. "Do you know where Atracta is?" he asked, trying to sound offhand and at ease, speaking again in the careful drunkard's manner.

"Isn't that the red-haired woman? I heard her tell the others she was off to the priest to get a 'dispinsary' for tomorrow. Whatever she meant," his aunt replied, still observing him.

Michael brightened a little. "Ah! But he won't give her one."

Miss Felicity Duff skipped in at the front door looking roguishly over her shoulder, although there was no one behind her. At the sight of the two of them she burst into shrieks of laughter, then girlishly clapped a mannish wrinkled hand to her mouth. It seemed to Michael that the people collected under his roof were without substance, no more than reflections in water that trembled and shuddered with each little puff of wind.

He felt a thousand miles away from everything. Time was passing, wreaths kept coming, Mr Younghusband the solicitor from Dublin had arrived, Kilrany came and went all day and, jaws steadily working, attended to awful duties.

"Now then, Aunt Virginia, that's you," he commented jovially as they screwed the coffin down. "Bilkin will surpass himself tomorrow," he warned his cousin again before going away for the night. "But do not despair."

"Why don't you put the poor old fellow out to grass?" Michael inquired absently.

"Not bloody likely!" came the bitter reply. "You little know what's coming after him."

Canon Bilkin's head drooped so much from the weariness of the years that it seemed to be attached to his breast rather than set on his shoulders. His voice was so weak that it hardly carried beyond the front pew where Michael sat with Kilrany. "Two and fifty years ago, almost to a day, I assisted at the burial of ah! little ah! Virginia Grahame," he began. "I was then but a curate at Cappoquin. Twenty-two years later, still in the same capacity, I was present when the Bishop ah! solemnized her wedding to that very gallant ah! gentleman . . ." He paused, racking his memory for the name, and gave it up. ". . . her husband. And today, my dear friends, in the presence of you all I shall bestow on her the priceless gift ah! of a Christian baptism. But first let us sing a hymn." The drone of his voice gave way to the whimper of the harmonium. Kilrany kicked his hassock and muttered.

Few of the mourners heeded the Canon. Everybody rose and in thin sad voices began to sing. All at once the congregation was mildly fluttered, like a meadow of long grass in a wind, and Michael looked round to see what was afoot. The first object to catch his eye was Atracta, who, apparently not content with defying Father Behan's edict, had crammed herself and the triplets into a pew reserved for the Family and occupied by Greatuncle Evelyn and Aunt Henrietta. A wonderful complacence illumined her wide face under its extraordinary hat. The second thing he saw, and what had caused the agitation, was none other than that enlightened sceptic Mr Browning, who in all the splendour of morning dress walked down the aisle and took his place beside Dulcie and Anne Louise. He had never been known to enter the church before except for his own wedding, and then only after he had tried and failed to arrange a proxy.

Even the impassive Kilrany, glancing round as well, slightly raised one eyebrow. As for Michael, this simple act of homage from one of his mother's old admirers moved him more than Mr Browning's letter had done, moved him to the depths of his heart: never again, he vowed, could he think altogether badly of him.

"Amen," everyone was singing.

" 'Man that is born of woman is of few days, and

full of trouble,' " Canon Bilkin began in a voice that creaked and sighed like a bed of rushes. " 'He cometh up like a flower and is cut down . . .' "

Mr Browning listened indulgently, lightly flicking the dust from his top hat. He had greatly enjoyed the effect of his appearance and now contemplated his own essential goodness with rapture. It struck him that he, and not the old dodderer with the yellow-silvery wisps of hair and the single open eye like an aged dog, was the one equipped to soothe, console and give rest to the heavy laden. Phrases from his letter to Michael slipped into his mind, and then phrases from other similar letters he had written over the long years and never forgotten, until his brain fairly hummed with the delight it took in itself.

". . . 'and man goeth to his long home,' " the Canon faltered.

Kilrany trained a ferocious glance on the old gentleman, daring him to collapse without his leave. He had himself laid down how the service should run and all this to-do about mourners in the streets and man's long home was simply a frill: the Canon had got seriously out of hand. Michael was pulling his sleeve and whispering like a naughty child.

"Did you ever hear how Bilkin was once debagged in Dame Street," he breathed, and snorted with laughter.

"Shut up, you ass," Kilrany hissed, angrily drying his ear. Even he had begun to feel the limits of endurance looming ahead. The congregation wailed out another hymn and the feeble old voice took up once more. Petals were falling like flakes of snow from the huge white peonies on the altar, which Kilrany had remembered were Virginia Duff's favourite flower. Then they were all in the open air and standing by the grave in a light but penetrating shower: a nice drop of rain and badly needed, Michael thought carefully, do the crops no end of good, there's no rain like May rain. Why, he thought, we are in May, well into May and Atracta was to have left at the end of April! He promised himself to look into the matter. At that moment they lowered the coffin and Atracta gave a screech, making as if to throw herself in with it but desisting on the brink, although no one had sought to prevent her. And then it was all over. The family and closer friends waited for the Canon to change his clothes and accompany them to the house, while the others one by one took their leave. To Michael's surprise, Mr Browning apparently deemed himself to be one of the latter group.

"Ah, my boy!" the philosopher said gaily, as he came up. "And so you got here too, did you? These things are sad, very sad." At the moment he was so much in love with himself that he could not fix his mind on any exterior thing. "How is your mother?" he continued, at his most charming and expansive. "A nice thing, this! The first time I have set foot in a church for twenty-three years, and she not there! Remember me to her, do."

He went on his way with a happy smile, which vanished as Atracta seized his hand and warmly shook it.

The occasion had mounted to her head like wine and she was busy shaking hands with all who crossed her path.

"Ballysimon should have been with us today," Michael remarked, staring stupidly about him. "He would have adored all this."

Kilrany took his cousin's arm in a grip of iron and dragged him away.

Twelve

On Atracta's right arm a little way above the wrist was an ancient burn the size of an egg. Years ago, stretching her hand out to turn a black pudding over in the frying pan, she had laid this arm in the way of a scalding jet from the kettle. Other people might have whipped the arm away, but Atracta's co-ordination was weak. She sensed that something was amiss, that some external factor was causing discomfort and even agony, but she was unable to pin it down. She stood there with the problem teasing her mind while the steam bit her flesh and a huge blister slowly began to form. From that day on she never cared as much for black puddings.

In the days that followed the funeral she found herself in a similar quandary. The pain was a spiritual one now but she was equally powerless to locate it. All she knew was that a great hurt was in her soul and that somewhere an ocean of tears waited to flow. It had started soon after they had led her Alf away to captivity in a foreign land, although not immediately. Gradually she had become aware of an aching void within which was more than the loss of consortium, sound government or even leather, painful as that loss might be. Then, returning from Crummagh one day with the triplets, she had encountered the fallen woman of the village with her bastard son and had made to pass on with the customary gracious nod that befitted Mrs Alfred Smith and the chatelaine of Georgetown. The woman stopped bang in her path, however, and began to chat without a shade of the deference owing to social and moral superiors.

"The boys are looking grand, God bless them," she had concluded, surveying the triplets with eyes that shone. "Ah, they're a credit to you all the same, Miss Moin."

This little exchange had greatly augmented her woe, she could not have said why. Then came the putting down of Mrs Duff and the exaltation of herself, and for a while it was as if life had burst into flower. The funeral was, after her own wedding, the finest moment of her career. Father Behan had readily agreed to her attending it and she had made over one of the mistress's hats with the help of a black woollen stocking, a raven's wing and some jet beads. It was the first time that she had ever placed a hat upon her head and it seemed an augury of improved status to come. In the church, conscious of the Divine approbation, she had classed herself with the Family and at the collation at the house afterwards she had felt it natural to do the honours of Georgetown. The little asperities that so often had cropped up in the past were seemingly now all smoothed away: her heart was full of love and forgiveness. But just as she was making for Canon Bilkin, a glass of madeira in her hand and a social smile on her lips, that kinsman of Master Michael's who always looked as if he were chewing gum very quickly had stalked up to her and in a dreadful voice had muttered, "Woman, are you out of your mind?" What in the name of God, Atracta would dearly have liked to know, could he have meant by that? She had retired in disorder to the kitchen and sat there puzzling over it, quietly crying and steadily drinking stout, with the hat tilted over one eye.

What hurt her more than anything, however, and caused her an uneasiness bordering on panic, was the conduct of the young master himself. Her belief that he was privately in love with her was almost beginning to wither away from sheer lack of sustenance to maintain it. A week after the funeral he had told her that while he sympathized with the difficulties of her position and would gladly do what he could to help she must please understand that she was now under notice again, and that she ought to apply herself to finding a new job.

Atracta spent hours in patient analysis of these words. That they did not mean what they appeared to on the surface went without saying, speech being given to man to cloak his thoughts rather than to reveal them. Could it be that he didn't like her? But then, why did he throw all those things and call her those names? Still, there was no getting round the fact that nothing she did was right. Kevin had broken the dining-room teapot one morning and she had to fall back on another, an old crock that the men used as an ashtray. It had gone in to breakfast cigarette ends and all and, honest to God, the row Master Michael kicked up, it was worse than a bagful of cats itself. There was no pleasing him and that was the truth, and he seemed if anything worse now the mistress was gone.

Atracta's invariable and infallible remedy for an unquiet mind was confession, communion and a tea party. The first two ingredients would have lost much of their healing power without the third, however, and a tea party at the present time she could not bring herself to face. It was not the fact of being a deceived woman and unmarried mother that distressed her, but of everyone knowing that fact and enjoying it. The thought of what her neighbours might be saying burned into her soul like acid. She did not even want to go to church, for fear of all those bright malicious eyes. Her one comfort was the rosary, which she would recite by the hour together in a flat singsong voice and with a completely vacant mind.

She was engaged in doing this one day when Nathaniel came in, having first knocked at the door, to ask if she would please mind sewing on a button for him. Atracta loved his courtly manners and simultaneously despised them, often remarking you'd never think Mr Waverley was gentry at all. For his part he prized Atracta for her simple faith and what he called her earth-quality, and would always stop for a pleasant word or two whenever their ways happened to meet.

So kind and responsive was he on this occasion that Atracta soon was blurting out her preoccupations and worries, as to an old friend. In particular, she repeated Michael's words of dismissal and anxiously asked him what he thought they could mean.

Nathaniel was up in arms at once, wholly on the side of the downtrodden victim. "I fear he means what he says," he cried. "But how monstrous! After all these years! And you with children!"

"Ah no, sir, he does not," Atracta replied. "Sure, he's always sayin' the like of that. But I was wonderin' now, would it have to do with me wages? Would he be shapin' to give me a raise?"

"But why?" Nathaniel asked, staring at her.

" 'Twas an idea that hit me," Atracta said wistfully.

"I don't think so, Atracta. I'm afraid not. No, I can't advise you to put any reliance on that. Most un-likely, it appears to me."

"But what else could it be, sure?" Atracta inquired, wrinkling her forehead.

"I am going to ask him," Nathaniel said firmly. "And if it comes to the worst, I'll have a word with a certain person I know." He bustled away, feeling agreeably righteous and important, and telling himself that the oppression of the honest but simple and uninstructed Irish peasant by the arrogant remnants of a decayed social system could hardly be equalled in darkest Africa. If there was one thing he loved in life, it was managing other people's business for them; and he saw that here might be a splendid chance of doing it.

Michael could find no mitigating feature in his English cousin at all. To begin with, as long as he was there Kilrany declined to set foot in the house, and Kilrany was the one man in Ireland whom Michael was always glad to see. The rest of the family after days of chattering together like a flock of starlings had, like starlings, all risen and flown away in a body; only Nathaniel stayed on, with his host counting the hours until his leave should be up and the ordeal over. But when that high day was on the verge of dawning, to Michael's despair Nathaniel procured a medical certificate saying he was unfit to travel, dispatched it to the BBC and, the picture of blooming health, settled down for a further spell. An inquiry as to how long the indisposition was scheduled to last was received in offended silence.

The conversion to Rome had provided young Mr Waverley with new and welcome opportunities for making a nuisance of himself, while he excelled in others that were old and tried. He believed he knew more than

Michael on every subject on earth, including farming and horses; and he set to work with a will to bring him to a more progressive frame of mind. Within a short time of his arrival he and the apostate Roger Buchanan had met and, as was inevitable, flown together like metal and magnet. Michael seldom came into the house nowadays but the pair of them were there, chattering about Gaelic culture, partition, James Joyce, the Irish martyrs in the dungeons of the North and heaven knew what besides.

What can be the matter with them? Michael often asked himself.

On the pretext that he could not be allowed to brood they plagued him to run hither and thither as they did, in order to meet "the people." He replied that he had met them, in plenty. Only, they riposted, on his vantage ground of old vested and unfair privilege, which was worse than no meeting at all. He readily conceded that no meeting at all would have suited him just as well, but did not see what could be done. This appeared to be what they hoped he would say. At once they hit back with the suggestion that he should invite a friend of theirs to dinner, a son of the people and a man of talent, if not genius, witty, cultivated, spiritual, a natural gentleman and lovable as only the Irish could be: who had given up a brilliant position in External Affairs to devote himself to furthering Irish culture.

"Who is he?" Michael demanded, wondering why he had not been aware of this paragon's existence.

"Mickey Hogan," Roger replied, not without a certain defensiveness.

"You're not serious!"

"Ah now, Michael," Roger pleaded, "that is the kind of reactionary defense mechanism we are trying to free you from." His eyebrows went up and down in his solemn round face all the time he was speaking, and his voice was pitched in the overwrought treble of a hound in full cry.

Michael fought stoutly and well, invoking the conventional decencies of mourning, the displeasure of all those whose invitations he had turned down on this score and his own unfitness to entertain genius; and finally menaced them with Atracta's food. Not even this could shake their resolve. "Just once, just see him once," they cajoled him, ruthless as any devout old ladies trying to save a soul. In the end they had their way: an evening was fixed and a written invitation extended to Mr Mickey Hogan, who sent word by Mr Foley that he didn't mind.

The invitation was for eight o'clock, and while for guests to have appeared at that hour would have been inconsiderate, if not barbarous, at half-past nine on the appointed evening Michael did begin to feel very much annoyed. He who had so strenuously opposed the whole dreary project was now the only one ready for it, and he was hungry and tired. Nathaniel was nowhere to be seen. At a quarter to ten Roger telephoned to say he was not coming. Michael asked hotly what the devil he meant by it and Roger answered in a cool businesslike manner that he meant precisely what he said. He put down the receiver without ceremony, while Michael stamped away to the dining room.

He found that an entire dinner, of grisly appearance, had been laid out on the sideboard in readiness and was now quite cold. There were four bowls of slimy brown soup with a thick wrinkled skin on it, four plates of salmon cutlets masked in congealed butter, four of roast lamb with a heap of burnt potatoes shovelled over each and four of rhubarb and custard. Every one of the plates had received the imprint of an immense black thumb, and the table was laid on a cloth, patterned with tea stains, that had been used for breakfast. Michael had looked out and decanted some claret, but there was no sign of it, nor of anything else to drink. The little clearing in the jungle made by Smith was lost forever under triumphant primeval forest.

Michael furiously rang the bell but nothing happened. It was now the very last lap of Atracta's sojourn at Georgetown and no doubt she had turned to sabotage as a reprisal. She would not have dared when frail potty little Mrs Duff was alive, any more than Mr Hogan would ever have crossed the threshold of the house: every day now things happened of which this could be said.

"And where the devil were you?" Michael asked, as Nathaniel slipped in with an air of guilty excitement.

"With Roger," he answered, tossing his curls.

"This bloody nonsense was Roger's idea," Michael said, "and he has just telephoned, cool as be damned, to say he isn't coming."

"Certain new facts have been brought to his attention," Nathaniel replied in a meaning voice.

Michael was not going to gratify him by asking what these were. "And where is your precious Hogan, may I ask?" he continued.

"Oh, you couldn't pin down a man like Mickey," Nathaniel replied with an airy wave of the hand. "There is something elemental about him, like the wind or a wave. Something, too, of the will-o'-the-wisp as it streaks over the bog."

"You do talk the most infernal tripe," Michael informed him, his heavy brows meeting in a way that boded little good for the will-o'-the-wisp when at last it should streak into Georgetown. "I'm going to have dinner. You please yourself."

"Rather bad manners, I should have thought," but Nathaniel was feeling hungry as well, and he set to work on the horrid fare with gusto.

Mr Hogan's car came weaving up the drive as the cousins were munching their way through the sticky roast lamb, and Nathaniel sped to the door to let the guest of the evening in. He was a fat red-faced man of about thirty, and he had brought with him a paler edition of himself whom he introduced as "the brother." His lateness was due, as he frankly explained, to his having forgotten all about the appointment.

"That is quite all right," Michael assured him. "So had we."

Mr Hogan looked at him, uncertain whether to take offence now or later. He had in fact thought of nothing else but the invitation ever since he received it and was late only because he had been drinking in order to give himself confidence and poise. The brother had been enlisted with a similar idea of support. The cool reception hurt him very much, and he dimly felt that he should have drunk either a great deal more or considerably less.

Confidence and poise, he reminded himself, however. With a light laugh he fell into one of the chairs at the table and tucked Nathaniel's napkin under his chin. It was curious that in spite of being firmly seated in a stationary chair he had all the sensations of driving at breakneck speed across country. He saw that he would have his work cut out to carry things off.

Confidence and poise, he murmured.

The brother sat down as well and coughed delicately behind his hand.

"Will you have salmon or lamb or both?" Michael asked the elder Mr Hogan. "Both are cold and both are vilely cooked."

Mr Hogan pondered the matter at length, his head on one side, with the air of a man who will not be rushed into momentous decisions. "I'll take the whiskey, so," he said at last. The table, he noted, was flying up to meet him.

"Arrah, Mickey, what ails ye?" the brother intervened in a low, shamed mutter.

"Give him the salmon, then," Michael said to his cousin. "And I think there's some whiskey in the sideboard."

"Nice little place you've got here," Mr Hogan proceeded affably; but his face clouded over in the next moment, as Nathaniel put the salmon in front of him. "What's this at all?" he cried. "Didn't I order rashers and eggs?"

"His own worst enemy," the brother moaned, with a gesture of despair.

"It is the chef's night out, I believe. Otherwise we should have been only too glad to accommodate you," Michael said. He made a little movement with his hand as Nathaniel poured the whiskey that Mr Hogan saw and rightly interpreted, with intense indignation, as a direction to go slow. "I hear you are deeply interested in culture, Mr Hogan."

" 'Deed then, I'm not, I hope I've more sense," Mr Hogan replied with asperity. "There's no money in culture at all. It's worse than the government service."

"You made a great hit with Mr Roger Buchanan, the solicitor. He is under the impression that you are going to help him organize a Drama Festival for Ballinaduff."

"That one? The old bletherer!" Mr Hogan chuckled. "I was only codding him along, the way you'd have to cod that class of a bloody eedjiot!"

The brother buried his face in his hands.

"Quite so."

Mr Hogan now perceived, in a moment of intense inward vision, that things stood very badly with him indeed. There was not the smallest hope of his dominating the party by confidence and poise: the question was rather the simple, clear-cut one of how long he could remain upright. He was travelling now not in a car, but in an aeroplane that banked and stalled and looped without mercy. The one fairly static object in the room was the luminous white front of Michael's shirt, and on this he fixed a stare so unwavering that the wearer ended by noticing it.

"Have I spilt my soup, or what's up?" he inquired amusedly.

These few words and the smile moved Mr Hogan to a sudden paroxysm of rage. "Culture, how are you!" he stormed, pounding the table with his fist. "I'll tell you the size of it, Mr Duff. Go into Ballinaduff any fair day you like and you'll see men there that can hardly write their names. And they're as full of money as the Bank of Ireland! And they'd buy you out of this four times over! Now!"

"That wouldn't be difficult," Michael remarked. He had a vivid sense of having lived through all this before, of every similar evening having closed in an identical way, as if the social life of County Drumanagh were but a long echoing hall of mirrors.

Mr Hogan bent quietly forward over the table and

lay very still, his cheek pillowed on the salmon cutlet.

"Honest to God," the brother said despondently as he helped Nathaniel to carry the patient out, "when Mickey's himself, our own father and mother couldn't read his mind. But let him take a few jars and he comes out with it all on his own, free gratis and for nothing."

Nathaniel blamed the fiasco on Michael. "If you hadn't worn that dinner jacket, all would have gone smoothly," he told him at luncheon next day. Michael had breakfasted early and rushed away to avoid a meeting.

"We still change for the evening in these benighted parts," he said.

"You don't! It was the first time since I got here," Nathaniel cried. "It was one of your ruses, typical. You deliberately set out to humiliate Mickey and make him feel uncomfortable."

"And that's how he does feel today, it wouldn't surprise me," their host responded, with a tigerish smile.

The door opened and Atracta came in with a registered letter, bearing it on a salver as in the palmy days of Smith and offering it to her employer as if it had been the freedom of a city. Having done this she retired immediately with the jaunty movements of hip that always accompanied her inner exultations.

"I wonder if this is for rates or income tax," Michael said idly. He was expecting trouble in connection with both. He opened the communication and glanced through it, and sat up with a choking cry as if stung.

"Holy smoke!" he vociferated. "Listen to this! From that prize idiot Buchanan. 'Atracta Moin (also known as Atracta Smith) versus Yourself. Blub-blub-blub wrongful dismissal blub-blub-blub clear breach of contract blub-blub-blub years of faithful service blub-blub-blub unequivocal reinstatement, with a reasonable solatium and an apology, failing which obliged seek redress . . .' " All at once he pulled himself up and grew gentle and calm. "This is your doing," he said, almost affectionately.

Nathaniel had grown very red in the face and was fidgeting with a spoon. "How could I stand indifferently by . . ." he began.

"And it's an ill wind that blows no one any good," Michael continued in the same tone. "My loss is England's gain. You'll pack and be out of this before tea."

"Michael, wait a minute. Let me explain . . ."

"And what's more you'll never set foot in Georgetown again," Michael purred.

"This will blow over. It is for your own good. All you have to do . . ."

Michael strode across the room and gave a tug to the bell, which came away in his hand, with no other perceptible result. He ran next to the door, crying out in a terrible voice, "Atracta!"

She was there, just outside, stooping with her ear to the keyhole. "I was only trying to visualize, were you waitin' on the pudding, Master Michael," she began in trepidation.

Michael tore Mr Buchanan's letter into tiny fragments and threw them at her. "Out! Away!" he commanded. "I don't want to see you ever again. Oh, you foolish, foolish woman!"

"God love you, Master Michael dear, I never had your brains and that's a fact." But the complacence in the yellow eyes belied the humble words.

"You haven't the brains of a retarded hen. Can't you see these fellows are making game of you? That they're laughing up their sleeves all the time?"

"Oh, Lord!"

"Don't believe him, Atracta!" Nathaniel called out. "The days are gone when you were at the mercy of the likes of him. Have faith in your people and Irish justice."

At the notion of Irish justice Michael broke into a happy laugh.

"Ah, Master Michael, to be laughing like that," Atracta said, with tender reproach. "And wasn't it the dear mistress's own last dying wish, that you should keep me here with my little ones?"

"WHAT?! Oh you unspeakable brute!"

"As God is my eternal judge," Atracta intoned, casting her eyes upward and laying one hand on her bosom, "my blessed lady's last words before moving on to her rest and her reward were that Master Michael should keep me with him, and leave me and mine in peace at the little cottage. And get the pantry door attended to," she threw in as an afterthought.

"Ah you . . . you creature!"

"I believe you, Atracta," Nathaniel said emotionally. "And as for you, Michael, you are making things worse for yourself. You forget surely that a witness is present."

"Before you are let give evidence, they'll find you in the ditch with your throat cut," Michael promised him.

"Threats! Aggravation! You attempt to intimidate me . . ."

"And barbarously mutilated." Michael specified a little, and Atracta fled with squeals of maidenly horror. The next idea that struck the goaded squire, however, caused his face to clear completely, as the rising sun will clear the mists of morning. "Don't forget to be out of here by four-thirty sharp pip emma," he remarked pleasantly. "Otherwise you won't have an inch of skin left on you." And, smiling, he left the room.

Kilrany was weeding the gravel paths in his rose garden when Mr Duff arrived, and painfully straightened up with a hand to the small of his back. "Ouch! What I need is a wife," he said, ruefully looking at the mile or so that remained to be done.

"You can't have Dulcie," Michael said at once. "But if you should care to make an honest woman of Atracta, I'll give her away myself and stand you a wedding breakfast."

Kilrany listened with close attention as Michael described the events that had led him to wishing his bondwoman might be settled in life, and interrupted only once, to ask: "Not Hogan the auctioneer?"

"No, his son. He used to be in External Affairs, but there was no money in it. He looks and behaves like a bookie."

"Nice company!" At the end of his cousin's narrative he said: "You had better see Mulally as soon as you can. Pity you tore the letter up like that."

"You don't take this seriously, Hugh?" Michael exclaimed in wonderment.

"Hm. I don't know. Talk to Mulally." For a moment Kilrany came as near to smiling as he was able. "Mulally fighting for you, and that besotted little Roger fighting for La Moin! Pretty work. But watch out that Mulally *does* fight," he added grimly, while his face returned to its habitual expression.

"Oh, mercy!" Michael groaned.

"We must look on the bright side," Kilrany proceeded gloomily. "Nathaniel has gone. And I presume we shall hear your wedding bells ere long now. Before you are grey-haired, at least."

"You won't hear them while that old bloodsucker is above ground."

"What! Do you mean to say you haven't heard the news? Why, no one speaks of anything else." Kilrany disclosed with morbid relish that Mr Browning, taking Zola as his precedent, was setting his cap at Bridget the Rougemain cook with a view to early marriage. "He ascribes it to his liberal views," he said, "but really he is worried about the grub. If Bridget left he'd never get anyone else. Funny that Dulcie didn't tell you."

Michael was stupefied. "But can it be true? I can't believe it. He's always so high and mighty about servants."

"Oh, I don't think he means her actual position to change at all. He was quoting Schopenhauer on the status of women. The whole idea of the 'lady' is a profound mistake, it seems. I don't often agree with Huns but I thought there was something in it. Now! Come on in and have a drink. Blowed if I'll do any more."

"Then I will be able to marry Dulcie after all!" Michael suddenly cried out.

"If you don't have to marry Atracta first. Talk to Mulally. Or," Kilrany said, making for the Castle at his greyhound's lope, "say the word and McCarthy shall put Buchanan down."

Thirteen

"Now d'ye see the way of it?" Mr Mulally asked with compassion.

There had been no need for Michael to follow Kilrany's advice and seek the attorney out. Mr Buchanan, forecasting the defendant's reaction to his letter, had prudently sent a copy of it to the legal adviser; and he, equally farsighted, had driven over to Georgetown that same evening. He had uphill work before him. For all that defendant's family had lived in the country above four hundred years he appeared as innocent as a baby in regard to its ways of thought. It had been hard enough to get him to see the genuine legal point: to realize that the "wrongful dismissal" alleged did not mean that Atracta was a competent servant unjustly discharged, but that she had been deprived of employment to which a contract written, spoken or implicit entitled her. Mr Mulally was not surprised to find Mr Duff hazy about the contract, for it was all of a piece with the well-nigh English fecklessness these old country families invariably displayed. Atracta's grandmother had come into the house as scullery maid, had been got into trouble by a groom and promptly married off to him on the orders of Michael's grandmother. They had one daughter, Lizzie, who also began work in the house as soon as she left school. By then the general decline in standards was already well underway and Lizzie occupied a grander place in the hierarchy than her talents justified, having reached at the time of her wedding to Patrick Moin, blacksmith, the rank of parlour maid. Both husband and wife perished soon afterwards through eating a meal of toadstools one Friday, the fish man having neglected to deliver in time for lunch; and Atracta, sole fruit of their union, was reared by a grandmother until she too left school and wandered into the house, to eat and drink her fill there and do just as little as she need. Michael had not the faintest idea what the original terms of her employment had been but confessed, with a shudder, that he could not remember a time when she was not there.

"A Ballinaduff jury," Mr Mulally had noted, knitting his brows, "is going to call that a contract."

But never mind all that legal stuff, he went on with a wave of his furry hand. The real hub of the matter was something quite irrelevant in the legal sense, and that was the dying woman's wish that Atracta should be kept on. That was what would weigh with a Ballinaduff jury, mother's darlings to a man, you might be sure, and what might even lead to exemplary damages; and the question his client should consider above all else was how he was going to diddle that jury.

"I keep telling you, there was no such thing," Michael said wearily. "My mother died of heart failure, in the throes of a choking fit. The doctor will tell you that much. Atracta just happened to be in the room. My mother had no time to express such a wish, even if it had occurred to her."

"How can you prove it?"

"How can Atracta prove the opposite?"

"Man alive," Mr Mulally said with emotion, "did you ever hear the expression, 'prefer the evidence?' You have your parties: their tales are diametrically opposed: one or the other is telling a thundering lie. The judge in summing up will say he 'prefers the evidence' of one of them, and if he gets the jury to agree, why, Bob's your uncle. And your other man's overboard. He's probably the one that's telling the truth, but there we are. Too bad! And I'm telling you, the evidence everyone but us is going to prefer in this case is the plaintiff's. Look-at! Simple honest god-fearing Irishwoman. Devout Christian, Blossom of the Sacred Heart, Legionary of Catholic Mothers, subscriber to *Vox Hiberniae*, never misses a Sunday or an obligation, weekly communicant. Newly, nay, wantonly! betrayed by Englishman. Unmarried mother through no fault of own. Three little mouths to feed. More on the way. Now thrown out on a harsh world," Mr Mulally cried, his voice rising and his eyes glowing, "suddenly and capriciously, in the hour of deepest affliction, by cynical landowner (Protestant) whose family has enjoyed three generations of faithful service from hers. In defiance of dead mother's last wish!" shouted Mr Mulally. "God Almighty! I'd call it open-and-shut!"

"But I've been sacking her for years, not just now," Michael objected, trying by the calmness of his tone to abate the other's frenzy. He did a little sum in his head. "I think I've sacked her twenty times, anyhow nineteen. It was the very first thing I did on coming of age. But she won't go. Words have no meaning for her. You tell her, 'You're sacked!' and she doesn't connect it with anything."

"You'll want to keep very quiet about all that," Mr Mulally advised. "Don't you see it bears out her claim that your mother wished her to stay? A Ballinaduff jury is going to reckon that the moment the poor lady is no more is when *you* start getting really tough." He picked up Mr Buchanan's letter and glanced rapidly through it again. "Ah yes, now, here. 'The Defendant often by his manner and in his actions showed that his feelings for the Plaintiff were warmer than are usual between Master and Servant,' " he read out. "What does that mean, pray?" And he looked at his young client over the tops of his spectacles.

Michael was beginning to feel giddy. "I can't imagine," he replied. "Why, I never saw her but I threw something at her."

"What?" screamed the lawyer.

"Oh, I never hit her. It was to let off steam. I had to do something."

"Why then does she think you had a special feeling for her?" Mr Mulally fired at him. "I can't help you unless you are frank with me, Mr Duff."

Michael heaved a prodigious sigh and looked round the room like an animal seeking a way of escape. How could Atracta be explained to a normal human being? "She is like that," he said helplessly. "It is the way she feels about herself. She is too stupid to know how stupid she is. She believes that she is wonderfully clever. If you knocked her down and dragged her round by the hair she would take it as a kind of tribute to her brains or her charm."

"A Ballinaduff jury is going to find that rather strange," Mr Mulally told his client very gravely indeed.

"And well it may," Michael replied.

Mr Mulally laid the letter down and placed the ends of his fingers together. "I hope you'll listen to me, Mr Duff," he said composedly. "I am a considerably older man than you. My father had the privilege of advising yours. I think I can get you out of all this for a couple of hundred pounds, and I am going to urge you, as strongly as I can, to let me do so."

"A *couple of hundred* pounds? And where am I to find them?"

"But don't you see, me dear man!" Mr Mulally said, abandoning his fine professional manner. "The alternative, which is fight, may well run you into a thousand or twelve-fifty, never mind your costs and hers. And never mind the infra dig."

"You can't mean it!" the defendant gasped.

"I can and I do."

"A thousand! Twelve hundred and fifty! It would break me. Are you really going to tell me that one cannot get rid of a completely useless, hopeless and impossible servant nowadays without being ruined?"

Mr Mulally confirmed that such was the disagreeable contemporary truth. "A Ballinaduff jury will say that, on the record, she could reasonably expect to pass her whole working life in your household," he pointed out, and Michael whimpered at the idea. "Furthermore the three children will be a serious handicap to her in her efforts to find a new place."

"She left us of her own accord to marry Smith," Michael said, melancholy coming into his face as it always did when he uttered that name.

"But didn't you take her back of your own accord?"

"Not really. She just flowed in and we were too lazy or too feeble to pitch her out. You know how life muddles along at Georgetown. Ah, but what's the use of talking? I'm done. You've a good idea of how things stand. We've been shipping more and more water every year and we were about to go down even before this happened. I'm waiting to hear the results of my appeal against the new rates: if it fails, I'm scuppered anyway. You say you'll get me out of this for two hundred pounds. I'd hardly dare put my name to a cheque for twenty-five at this minute, and that's the long and the short of it." He leaned back in his chair, somehow refreshed and relieved by the sheer hopelessness of it all.

"And you never thought of getting out of this benighted land?" Mr Mulally asked. "If I were your age . . ."

"I think of almost nothing else."

"And why don't you? 'Tisn't the place for the likes of you, Mr Duff. We are ruled by hooks and hypocrites, though for God's sake don't repeat that," the lawyer said, tucking the letter away in his case. "Holy Fly! isn't that the Angelus ringing? I'll be late for me next appointment." It was his confraternity evening, he never missed. "I'd best have a word with Buchanan, so. Mind you, I'm not hopeful. When a man turns his coat he usually does it thoroughly. We'll see."

"How on earth is Atracta going to manage?" Michael asked as he accompanied the lawyer to the door. "She has no money either, that I know of."

"Man dear," Mr Mulally said with an awful tender pity, "she's not going to need any." And on this note of doom he took his departure.

Michael turned his steps to the drawing room, thinking to calm himself with half an hour of the television. It was the first really hot day of the year and hence he was not a little surprised to see that a big fire was lighted there, burning a great deal better than was its wont. Even as he stood wondering at it Atracta slipped into the room with an apronful of dry logs, with which she prepared to stoke the flames still higher. He felt the old fascination and horror creeping over him at the sight of her there before him, assuaged, important and rehabilitated.

"I've been talking to Mr. Mulally, Atracta," he began.

Atracta looked at him fondly, as if their little contretemps must somehow draw them all the closer together.

"Do you remember the new Pope's cyclamen?" he continued. "About perjury being a mortal sin? And how you couldn't get absolution from Father Behan for it, but would have to go to the Bishop himself?"

"I do of course, Master Michael," she said, thinking this a queer old way for gentry to talk.

"And what is perjury, Atracta?"

"God love you, Master Michael, how would I know?"

"It is a lie spoken on oath. When you take an oath in court and give evidence before a jury every single word you utter has to be true."

"Go 'way!" she exclaimed, smiling broadly. "Is that right, Master Michael? And at the heel of the hunt you mightn't win!" She looked at him with indulgence, regarding his statement as so much idle talk.

"No, indeed, you might not. Well, I'm going up to see Father Behan just now," he told her. "I shall ask him to explain it to you, so that you never repeat that wicked lie about my mother."

"God rest her!" Atracta intoned. "But Father Behan isn't there at all just now, he's out sick. There's only a timperate priest in charge."

These words afflicted her employer with a chill sense of fate closing in. "A temporary priest?" he echoed. "Father Behan ill? What is the matter with him? Where is he?"

"There was a grand long name they gave to his trouble," Atracta replied, "but it meant no more in the world than he was wrong in the head. They do be sayin', 'twas the confirmation class that regulated him. And he's in the city now, in a home, till they see can he ever come back or not."

He looked at her then, this creature who was going to break him, as if he saw her for the first time. She was one of those things like a clubfoot or a black skin that Heaven, moving in its mysterious way, landed you with, that you could never escape, that shadowed the whole of your life. He noted an access of animality in the wide face and knew, with horror, what it portended. *There will be more triplets* . . . Virginia Duff's small voice echoed in the great shabby room. How much he missed her, how much had been altered and how quickly; what monstrous things had taken heart from her disappearance!

"Go away, Atracta," he said. "Try to keep out of sight. I might so easily kill you," he explained.

Atracta smiled happily at the threat, seeing in it only a further proof of his attachment to her person. "Ah, you're gas, Master Michael," she laughed. "But I came in to ask you, would you not give me the little chist of drawers all the same? The wan above that would fix so sedately in me parlour?"

Michael turned his back on her and walked hurriedly to the window. "It is simply not true," he said in low urgent tones, thinking aloud. "I'm dreaming this. Soon I shall wake. It is simply not conceivable that this . . . this . . . this freak should stand there, after all she has done and is doing, and coolly beg for a chest of drawers."

"Sure, you'd never miss it, Master Michael honey," came in the whining voice, "and Patrick's after destroyin' the little one I had with the blowlamp Tomo gave him."

"Get out of the room," he entreated her. "And do it fast."

Atracta withdrew, groaning and muttering. Her employer stood there looking out over the countryside. Of all the different faces it put on, the one it wore this evening was the most lovely, most rarely seen, when earth and sky shimmered in a kind of gold-and-silver haze touched lightly here and there with rose or lilac tints. It seemed as ever to be laughing at him, mocking him, telling him *"But I am not Ireland, Atracta is!"* He turned away with a shiver and, for something to do, switched on the television. Once again there were pictures of jubilation in some African state, the frantic song and dance, the capsized vehicles, the flames, the flowers. It seemed as if nothing else ever happened anywhere nowadays. Tonight, however, he no longer participated in the joyful sense of liberation, no more saw in the chaos a hope of freedom and new life for himself: all the future appeared now to lie in the stumpy hands of Atracta. A multitude of Atractas was emergent in every part of Africa, in every corner of the world, and invincible in their stupidity would sweep all before them. A global saturnalia was in train and would never slacken or falter until it had annihilated him and his kind forever. The people who in some mysterious way had known how to check it and hold it off, such as his mother or Ballysimon, all were dead or dying. The floodgates were open and no living force could shut them.

He switched off again and walked back to the window, thinking sadly of the happiness of the afternoon when Kilrany had revealed Mr Browning's lunatic but providential purpose to him. Vistas of joy he had never before dared contemplate had opened in a blaze ahead, obliterating every care, making light of every danger. Who said you couldn't live on love? It was precisely love, he had thought, that you could live on, better than on anything else. For a delirious spell he had really felt as if he were married to Dulcie already. Then had come the interview with Mr Mulally and darkness fell on the world again, an unrelieved pitch blackness without a ray of hope in it anywhere.

When at last he went up to bed he noticed that the fungus was growing on the wall again, more evilly luxuriant than ever.

Fourteen

MR ROGER BUCHANAN sat in his newly painted newly
furnished office, babbling away at his new tape recorder.
He was savouring together the two keenest pleasures in
his life, the one, topmost, of battling for a noble idea,
the other, unconscious but if anything the keener, of
annoying his father. Although he was not aware of it
his simple filial hatred of Major Buchanan had been the
chief motivating force of his life. It had propelled him
into the national university and the firm of Rooney,
Rooney & Rooney, Solicitors, whereas family tradition
required him to join the Brigade of Guards and die, if
it could at all be arranged, on the field of battle. It next
had whirled him away to London to join the Labour
Party, make speeches in Trafalgar Square, to march

hither in protest against this and thither in support of that, write articles in *Tribune* and the *Statesman* and marry a black barmaid called Nellie Rose Fernandes. It had brought him back, shortly after Nellie Rose had run off with a black bookie called Rossignol McCarthy, to serve the people of Ireland within shouting distance of that symbol of bygone oppression, the Buchanans' ancestral home. Major Buchanan never spoke of these things or heard them mentioned but his face would turn a curious mottled blue.

"Would you mind just playing that back?" Mr Buchanan said courteously to the tape recorder. He switched it over but nothing happened. What was amiss? He was not yet used to these strange new things. Rooney, Rooney & Rooney had done all their recording very slowly by hand, using a pen somewhat like a quill. He switched the thing off and then on and gave it a cross little smack but still nothing came of it.

Someone walked into the outer office and stood fidgeting there, coughing and breathing hard. Mr Buchanan waited for Miss Maguire to knock on his door and announce the visitor; but again nothing happened and he recollected, with an irritation that he at once deplored, that it was Corpus Christi and Miss Maguire had gone to Mass. He was considering what steps he should take in the matter when Mr Mulally put his head round the door, wearing a radiant smile.

"Have you a moment at all?" he asked cheerily.

"Well . . . hardly. I'm very busy at present," Mr

Buchanan replied, although in fact Moin *versus* Duff was the only case he had.

"Lots of work, eh? That's right," Mr Mulally said. He was aware of the real position. "Ah, but you wouldn't drive me away. I'll not delay you long," and he bore down on the visitor's chair with the clear intention of occupying it.

"If it is about Michael Duff . . ."

"It is, of course. Who else would it be?" Mr Mulally sat down and to Mr Buchanan's acute annoyance lit a cigarette. "I'm going to give you some fatherly advice," he said pleasantly.

"Most improper . . ."

"This is the kind of little pie a young gentleman like yourself should keep out of," Mr Mulally proceeded, unmoved. "Conspiracy! Perjury! 'Tisn't at all what we look to see a Buchanan mixed up in."

"Intolerable!" Mr Buchanan cried. "How dare you make such a false wild wicked assertion about my client and myself? And blow the Buchanans. I will not have the Buchanans thrown up at me."

"Me client has no money," Mr Mulally continued, without heeding him, "and yours has no case. Now!"

"No case, Mulally?" Mr Buchanan said awfully. "No case?" He leaned back in his chair and looked down his nose at the intruder. "I am a highly intelligent, responsible and qualified woman," he stated, affecting a sophisticated nasal drone like that of a London barrister he knew. "I am respected by neighbours and parish priest.

As cook, housekeeper and sole manageress of an establishment formerly employing eleven inside I may justly claim to be in a class of my own. My value to the decayed gentleman who employs me is clear from the fact of his snapping me up again directly my marriage comes to an unfortunate conclusion. The aforesaid decayed gentleman manifests, furthermore, his regard for me in a hundred and one little intimate ways. Yet what happens? Not content with paying my wages ever more sporadically he suddenly, without warning, without explanation and for no reason, turns me out. With three small children already born to me, not to speak of the precious little new life on the way. In defiance of the last words of his own mother, to whom I have always been more daughter than servant. Holding me up to the mirth and the scorn of the locality. No case? We shall ask for seven hundred and fifty pounds."

Phew! Not too bad, Mr Mulally thought.

"On that count, mark you," Mr Buchanan said instantly. "On the count of wrongful dismissal. There remains the question of my ruined life and lost expectation of marriage."

O Sacred Heart! thought Mr Mulally. "You'll hardly hold me client to blame for the bigamy?" he asked, casual and amused.

"We do not refer to the bigamy at all," Mr Buchanan said loftily. "A worthy local man offers me his name, care and protection. Or rather, did so offer them before this grievous hurt to my reputation and standing."

O Sacred Heart! thought Mr Mulally again. His own heart missed a beat. "Ye'll not get a penny piece," he observed genially. "Look-at! I am one of the first gentlemen of the neighbourhood. Me family has lived here these four hundred years. In better times I and me fathers before me gave great employment to the people, not to speak of christening mugs, beer and beef at harvest and dances at the New Year. I meself am known as a man of truth and probity"—a shade of disapproval crossed Mr Mulally's intelligent Gaelic face as he uttered these words—"and if I declare your whole case to be a pack of bloody lies, 'tis my word will be taken."

"Just because I am a simple woman of the people!" Mr Buchanan exploded, turning scarlet.

"Man dear, did you talk to her yet?" Mr Mulally inquired with friendly solicitude.

"I have naturally seen her," Mr Buchanan said with confidence. "But she was brought here by a cousin of Duff's, who had acquainted himself with the facts and helped her to present them acceptably. A most humane and interesting man. Why do you ask?"

"Curiosity," Mr Mulally replied with a grim smile. "To come down to brass tacks, Buchanan. Me client will offer fifty pounds without any kind of admission on his part."

"Fifty pounds!" Mr Buchanan exclaimed in his throbbing treble. "My life is ruined, my heart broken, and you offer me fifty pounds! I thought you said we had no case," he added ironically.

"You've not. And the kind of damages you want means sessions, with High Court judge and procedure. It's fifty to one, I'd say, the judge'll throw you out. I'm putting me cards on the table, Buchanan. It's because of that odd chance or two he might just send you to a jury and because I know, as you don't know"—here Mr Mulally's voice trembled and a look of such anguish came over the plastic features that Mr Buchanan flinched a little in spite of himself—"what a Ballinaduff jury is capable of, that we make any offer at all. And it's the last. So now!"

Sounds of a kettle being put on for tea and a cigarette being lit in the outer office denoted the completion by Miss Maguire of her religious duties and a preparation for her secular ones. On hearing them Mr Buchanan at once became very formal and businesslike.

"Any offers you have must be made in writing, and will appear in the pleadings," he said with importance. "This whole discussion is highly unorthodox."

"Ah, don't give me that! We're not in the Temple. If that client of yours has a grain of sense in her head, or if you can knock one into it, take the fifty and let the thing drop. No good," Mr Mulally freely admitted, "ever came of going to law."

"Mr Mulally, I propose to conduct this case in accordance with right procedure and etiquette and with the interest of my client as sole consideration," Mr Buchanan said, in cool ascendency tones. "I have nothing to add, except to wish you a good morning."

The tape recorder that had been quietly holding its peace all this while now decided to intervene. "Alistair Greville Robert Buchanan, you have been found guilty of a crime for which . . . but one penalty," it babbled excitedly. Blushing, Mr Buchanan made ineffectual little jabs at such parts of the instrument as he thought were responsible for this breach of his confidence but it continued unmoved, determined to have its say. ". . . taken from thence to the place of . . . by the neck until you are . . . may the Lord have mercy on your . . ." At last it had done.

"Testing, testing, don't you know," Mr Buchanan said brightly, avoiding Mr Mulally's eye. Mr Mulally looked at him, his lips pursed in a soundless whistle. "There would appear to be a fault in the mechanism. Or it may be that I need practice."

"I'd say you're great," Mr Mulally said dazedly. "Well, I'm away. I'll not take up more of your time, with all there is on your mind." He went away still whistling noiselessly and full of dark foreboding, life having taught him early on that nutty colleagues were the worst kind you could possibly have to deal with.

Young Mr Duff was in little better case. Much as it irked him, he had gone to the length of calling at the parish house and appealing to the present incumbent for help. His story sounded, as any narrative occupying itself principally with Atracta would do, totally insane; but he ploughed on through it, concealing nothing, explaining nothing, asking nothing, censuring not at all. At last he came to the end of it and sat there, wearily looking at the curate in charge without any great hopes of him.

"Certainly the woman would appear to be poorly instructed," Father Sweeney said hesitantly. He would only be in Crummagh a short time and was damned if he wanted trouble.

"She's quite mad," Michael answered. "But she always did as Father Behan told her."

"That poor good man is none too well himself," Father Sweeney remarked with a sigh. "I know the Bishop was anxious for him. There's more work in a parish like this than you might suppose. I'd like to help you, all right, Mr Duff, but I don't just see what I can do." He looked kindly and sympathetically at the young man while his agile brain ran over the dozen or more aspects, all unfavourable, that any action taken by him might be held to wear.

"You couldn't speak to her?"

"I could not, Mr Duff, unless she came out with it first herself," Father Sweeney told him sadly. "There'd be talk. I'd look to be interfering in a legal matter and, anyway, the parish would think I should take her side."

"But I'm not saying you should tell her to chuck it," Michael pleaded. "I merely thought you could tell her what perjury is. I told her myself and she supposed I was pulling her leg."

"The woman is going to the courts with a case," Father Sweeney said, more dismally yet. "I can know nothing of the case. You say she means to commit perjury. If I talk to her about perjury I will seem to be taking your view. She could complain of me. And there'd be talk." The possibility of talk was the final argument against anything for Father Sweeney. Seeing the despair in the young man's face he added consolingly, "If indeed she commits perjury she'll be bound by the Bishop's ruling. And although I can't speak for his Lordship, the matter of restitution would surely come in, if you had suffered."

"But she'll never know she has committed it!" Michael groaned. "She has no idea of anything at all!" What was the use of trying to explain?

He rang up Kilrany. "I am going out to get drunk," he said.

"Capital," Kilrany answered. He knew the hour was grave when Michael resorted to the telephone. "I'll come along and keep you at it."

They met an hour afterwards in the Ballinaduff Arms, with the resolute bearing of men who approach an enterprise of importance. It was rarely that they broke out but they made a conscientious job of it when they did so, and followed an invariable procedure, hallowed by memory and convenience. The Ballinaduff Arms was the first place of call, being a country inn of great respectability, run by a retired admiral and as a rule full to overflowing with cheery red-faced sportsmen. From here they moved on to the Station Hotel, a bare three miles from the station, which was owned by a cockney and with its garish neon lighting had a flavor of the Edgware Road. Thereafter they ceased to be particular and, beautifully, magically estranged from their environment, moved here and there as blithe fancy dictated, to Mulligan's, Delaney's, to Flood's by the mill and O'Hooey's up the mountain, controlled, dedicated, a little formidable and completely happy. Neither suffered the least ill effect on the morrow.

There was to be a fair in Ballinaduff on the following day and men and cattle already stood about the square outside the Arms, as if in a practice battle. A light rain fell and the greyness of the sky together with the dejected appearance of man and beast, the squalor of the buildings around and the piles of dung on the road, offered a spectacle of unrelieved misery. Somewhere near at hand a fiddle was squeaking away like a basket of kittens. The cousins looked on awhile at the crowd over the frosted glass in the parlour window. From such countrymen as these, their faces blank and stony as they lauded their stock and decried that of others, Michael supposed, would be drawn the twelve good men and true who would prefer Atracta's evidence to his and sink him for ever. This notion was too horrifying to bear alone and he communicated it to Kilrany.

"Try and put the whole thing out of your mind," Kilrany counselled him. "That is the advice they give in the condemned cell, I believe." He led him away from the window and back to the bar and, jaws working, heard Michael's account of the development *in re* Moin *versus* Duff since last they had met. "Frightened of his shadow, the usual thing," he commented, with regard to Father Sweeney. "But you'll have to mind Mulally, and buy the hag out."

"With what, for instance? I can't pay my bills."

"Isn't there a wood, or part of one, you could sell? Timber's fair at present. Or one of the fields?"

"Damned if I do," was the spirited reply. "When I go, I go. There'll be no cutting up and parcelling out."

" 'The boy stood on the burning deck,' " Kilrany jeered. "He got his trousers burnt, all the same. Now I think we will have more, even a lot more, to drink."

Their thoughts were running clear and fast by the time they took themselves along to the Station Hotel.

"Only two men in the world could save me!" Michael cried with irrepressible glee. "One's in quod and the other in a bin!" Kilrany emitted the brief harsh bark which coming from him signified extreme amusement. Then the old melancholy returned to Michael's face and lowering his voice he asked, "How did he do it, Hugh? What was his secret?"

Kilrany caught on at once. "He faced facts," he said, "and acted on them. That kind of English do. And they made the old shop. It was chucked away by the other kind, who think you can make silk purses out of sows' ears." A look of detestation accompanied these words. "By the cousin Nathaniels."

Michael heaved a sigh. "I think he was a truly great man," he said wistfully. "Only, how in the name of God *could* he . . ." It was the abiding mystery.

Elsie the proprietress of the Station Hotel had three styles of greeting, the cheery smile for All, the bright smile for those tabulated by her as Nice People and a blinding semaphore flash for the nobs, which broke uncontrollably forth as the two young men came into her bar. Everything about her was bright, from her alarmingly auburn hair to her spangled shoes. Brightness indeed was the whole end and aim of her spiritual life: her bottles and glasses were dazzling and she was forever devising some means, a string of coloured lights, a huge vase of paper flowers, a fan glued to the wall, for enhancing the general effect of scintillation. The latest of them was a stand of post cards of Irish scenes, portrayed in vivid and alluring colour.

"Brightens the place up," she pointed out when the salutations were over and Michael complimented her on her taste.

"There's Bob's little detached residence," Kilrany remarked, indicating an enormous grey castle romantically set on the shore of a lake. "He's selling, I hear. To a Hun. Tried throwing the place open to the public. Only got eleven and sixpence in the whole season and some bugger pinched a Waterloo sword. Sorry, Elsie, I mean, some distinguished visitor. Oh, and pray look at Brian's slum!" he went on, pointing to another castle which coyly peeped from a wreath of emerald trees. "Mother Church has her mittens on it, they say. This is really all rather jolly. Like a graveyard."

"And here, by God, is Atracta!" Michael said, his

voice weak with laughter. There was something tremendous bubbling and flashing inside him all at once, as if he were on the brink of a staggering illumination of the soul, or an epileptic fit. He was looking at the picture of a simple barefoot Connemara girl, demurely leading an ass laden with turf from the bog. "And there go I," he said, pointing to the ass and laughing so much he could hardly stand.

"No need to behave like a foreigner," Kilrany reproved him. "Bless me! Here's our gay metropolis." The card depicted the Ballinaduff square they had just left but now as smiling in the sun, the houses washed in gentle colours, the fringe of chestnut trees in flower, a line of blue hills appearing far away over the tilted roofs of the town, all bathed in contentment and peace. "What's more," he exploded in sudden fury, "it can bloody well look like that. I've seen it bloody well look like that."

"So've I," Michael said, tears of laughter in his eyes. "I've seen it bloody well just like that."

"Let's go," Kilrany said, ferociously swallowing a drink at one gulp and walking out of the bar with Michael at his heels, while Elsie mewed brightly after them in her disappointment.

"You'd better let me drive," Kilrany said.

On the way to Delaney's Michael burst out in helpless giggles again. "The only sane man in Ireland, in a bin!" he cried, but Kilrany was no longer amused.

It was only when they were in Delaney's fume-heavy den with a purple-faced countryman asleep on the floor at their feet that revelation burst on Michael and all but swept him away. It was not merely that he was going to put Georgetown on the market and clear out, or even that the approaching union of the philosopher at Rougemain and his cook removed the last obstacle to marriage with Dulcie. Ever since the talk with Father Sweeney these ideas had been slowly working in his mind. It was that the door of his prison had been thrown open, the road to bliss unbarred, by that plague and torment of his life Atracta who in all witlessness had provided him with what he had always wanted, a legitimate sufficient excuse for laying his burden down and living to please himself. He loved Atracta then: he loved her not in spite of her greed and cunning and duplicity but because of them. Whether it was the contrast of the charming portrayal of Ballinaduff with the sullen sodden aspect of the reality, or the large unaccustomed amount of drink he had swallowed, he had a sudden intense vision of his country as completely and reassuringly dual and ambiguous, with all that was most apparently frightful in it working sweetly and harmoniously toward infinitely desirable ends. For the first time in his life he felt passionately at one with his native land, not merely rallying to it when someone said the things about it he said himself, but feeling Irish to the core of his being, even to finding a twisted pleasure in the sight of Kilrany calmly drinking beside him in innocence and trust, happily unaware of his traitorous intentions. He beamed fatuously over the top of his glass.

"So you're going to hop it," the latter remarked, looking at him.

"How did you know?" Michael asked in astonishment.

"Not difficult," Kilrany replied. "If you see that kind of poggle bliss on our kind of face these days, it means emigration."

"Do you blame me?"

"I do not. Wish I was going too." Kilrany paused, fiddling with his glass, strangely hesitant. "Everything's up, anyway," he muttered. "I didn't like to tell you. This is the last time I could come out with you on a spree."

It was an appalling tale he had to tell. Only two days before old Canon Bilkin had climbed into bed and declared that nothing in the world should ever get him out of it again, nothing, did they understand? He simply lay there with his eyes shut, a flagon of barley water and a volume of Horace beside him, and repeated his announcement in a feeble monotonous chant while Kilrany paced up and down the room with the frenzy of a caged lion, storming and pleading and threatening. For no replacement could be found: no other man was prepared to take on a tiny dwindling parish with an enormous mouldering Rectory in a part of the country that itself was fast emptying out; and Kilrany—here was the bloodcurdling part—would henceforth minister to the spiritual needs of the neighbourhood in the capacity of a lay reader. He had been secretly and doggedly and bitterly preparing himself for the duty for some time past.

"And will you even preach sermons?" Michael asked, sobered, wellnigh stunned, by the news.

"Yes," Kilrany replied, with Roman simplicity.

After a shocked silence, "I've been at you all afternoon with these stupid little worries of mine," Michael said in a low humble tone, "fussing about Sweeney and Mulally and Atracta and God knows what, and there all the time you . . . you . . ." His voice shook and, overcome, he seized Kilrany's hand.

"You're behaving like a foreigner again," said Kilrany sharply, drawing the hand away. "No good ever came of it. Finish your whiskey up and have some more."

Fifteen

ATRACTA had been the death of her mistress and had played her full part in bringing about Father Behan's collapse; and she was now exerting herself on behalf of Mr Roger Buchanan.

It was their second meeting and their first tête-à-tête and it was held of course in Mr Buchanan's newly rented newly furnished newly painted rooms. The man who faced his client across the newly equipped writing table, however, was no longer quite the same as he who had defined his position and point of view so eloquently to Mr Mulally. That man had been neatly dressed and his docile hair had clung to his head like a silken cap. This man's tie had worked itself round to a harbour under his ear, and his hair stood up in fretful spines. That man had spoken copiously and buoyantly, in a high tremolo. This one frequently broke off with a gesture of utter weariness, even of despair, and his voice became something between a whisper and a croak. The change showed itself above all in the mazed expression of the solemn owlish eyes; they were eyes which all too clearly had looked on things it is not good for men to see. In short, Mr Buchanan was no longer anything like as happy as he had been about Moin *versus* Duff.

For her part Atracta was not at the height of her mental powers. A wild terror of anything strange, anything unknown, was one of her chief characteristics, and to say that of late Master Michael was behaving unaccountably was to put it very softly indeed. Going into the office one morning to inform him the process server was there again, desirous this time of serving a writ for the nonpayment of rates, she was hailed with a broad, almost affectionate smile. It made her flesh creep at any time to see Master Michael smile, as it looked for all the world then as if the portrait of the father had come alive and was walking the house, even one day might open its mouth and put a long curse on her for the silence she had kept up all these years about that blessed shooting; but never before had a smile of the son's been aimed in her direction. Startled, she had glanced over her shoulder to see who might be standing there behind her and saw but empty space. That smile, she fearfully grasped, was intended for her; and her young employer had followed it up with the terrifying words, "Ah, Atracta, you're a decent old skin after all!" What could be behind it, what devilment, what mischief to her and hers could Master Michael be plotting? And it was not on the one occasion only that he behaved in this ominous way. His eyes sparkled now whenever he caught sight of her and often he would break into a merry laugh. He would say extravagant, horrifying things such as "What would I do without you?" or "You'll never know how much you've meant to me," accompanying these remarks with that same mysterious dreadful smile. He never swore, shouted or shied things at her nowadays. He was clearly up to something diabolical and the worry of it preyed on her mind night and day, causing her to arrange her thoughts with appreciably less than her wonted lucidity.

Mr Buchanan had received no acknowledgment of his opening letter beyond Mr Mulally's personal and highly unorthodox call. Accordingly he had written again to say that if there were no answer forthcoming within fifteen days of date he should begin proceedings without further ado. Now he was trying to get from Atracta a statement of the whole affair in a concise and factual form that could go to counsel for opinion. At their previous interview she had merely sat by sucking a peppermint toffee while Nathaniel described her situation and, ably as he had done it, Mr Buchanan now required it all over again in Plaintiff's own words. He had fully expected that thanks to centuries of brutal oppression and the denial of elementary human rights Atracta's capacity for expression might fall something short of what was needed. At Rooney, Rooney & Rooney he had ever explained the vagaries and foibles of the clients to himself in this way. It might be that they could not write their names, it might be they had poisoned off the four people that stood between themselves and a farm, it was certain they had no idea of what truth might be, but for Mr Buchanan all was lumped together as the result of alien misrule. For Atracta's way of looking at things and the chaotic private world she inhabited, however, he was but ill prepared. It took him three-quarters of an hour to elicit from her such vital information as her name and address: her age she did not know. Worse was to follow when he came to the matter of the case itself. There was, for example, the important question of the local citizen who had offered name, fortune and protection, only to withdraw this offer on hearing of Atracta's dismissal. It was essential for Mr Buchanan to know who the citizen was and what, either by mouth or by pen, had been uttered in the way of proposal and of withdrawal of the same. Atracta readily disclosed that the suitor was Tomo the Georgetown handyman, but could produce nothing in substantiation of her claim to have been wooed and jilted.

"He never said annythin' at all," she said. "Sure, what would he say?"

Her case appeared to depend on two, to her mind relevant material and sufficient, facts, namely that Tomo drove the bull into her kitchen one Monday morning and that he gave the chiseller a blowlamp to play with, with which said chiseller had promptly ruined a chest of drawers, the wedding gift of Plaintiff's aunt. What, Atracta demanded with the courteously restrained triumph of a chess player calling "Mate!" could the first have meant but that Tomo was after her and what the second, only he'd changed his old mind?

Mr Buchanan put a hand to his brow. "Now, madam," he said. He used this term to avoid the delicate matter of addressing a mother of triplets as a single lady, and Atracta kicked like a rabbit with glee every time he did so. "Now, madam, this will not do. We must have more to go on if we are to convince the court that by Duff's action you lost the chance of a happy and honourable marriage."

"Is it marry that one?" Atracta exclaimed in astonishment. "Sure, I'd never do that. And anyway, I'm married to Mr Smith."

Mr Buchanan patiently cleared his throat. "I'm very much afraid the law says you are not."

"The law!" Atracta smiled serenely on him. "Father Behan says I am."

In this she spoke the truth. After considering the details of all Smith's previous marriages Father Behan had declared that each was invalid in canon law, that accordingly Smith had been free to marry her and that, since he had done so in the prescribed Catholic forms, she was his true lawful and indissolubly wedded wife.

Mr Buchanan saw that his client would be enough for the afternoon without embarking on canon law, and

(214)

he continued: "In that case, madam, why do you raise the matter of Tomo at all?"

"I thought I'd give the chancer one for himself," Atracta replied.

Her legal adviser vigorously struck a paragraph or two out of the neatly written notes in front of him, and laboured on. "Let us begin with the actual dismissal," he suggested. "I understand it was by word of mouth. When did Michael Duff first tell you to go?"

"O Lord!" Atracta said, clapping a hand to her mouth and piously looking to heaven. "I'd hardly know that. 'Twas at the big party the mistress gave for him, that time he was twenty-one. He came at me in the kitchen with a glass in his hand. He'd a sup or two taken, God love him."

Mr Buchanan had attended this same party and now could feel his brain commencing to wobble. "But that must have been six years ago, or more!" he cried.

"Is that right?" Atracta wondered. "How the time does run, all the same. And ourselves all heading for eternity!"

"But you've been there ever since! You didn't go!"

"I did not, of course," Atracta agreed. "Sure, where would I go? The little ones were only after comin'." It crossed her mind that her attorney was not half as brilliant as Mr Waverly had made out. "Master Michael was often tellin' me go away," she explained. "He'd get a bad day or the mistress would rile him, and he'd come out with it on me. But I didn't mind him, not the smallest bit in the world. He was only talkin'."

Mr Buchanan clutched his head. "But I gather, on this occasion he is not 'only talking,'" he said, panting a little. "Now: kindly put out of your mind all thought of hasty words that may have been spoken over the years and tell me when, *when*, WHEN! Michael Duff first gave you formal notice to leave on this occasion and no other." A mad thought rose in his mind that perhaps it could be arranged, even now, for Mulally and himself to swap over clients.

Atracta pondered, her cat's eyes squinting a little. "I know! 'Twas on the first day of Friday," she exclaimed then, in triumph. "I'd to get Mass and he wanted his breakfast. 'Twas that set him workin'."

"I think you may mean the first Friday of the month," Mr Buchanan informed her, articulating with difficulty. "But of what month?"

Atracta's wide pink face lit up. "The month Alf came home," she said softly.

"Very well, then. That, I believe, was April. Duff gave you notice on the first Friday in April last. Come, we are doing famously! Now, madam, how long a notice did he give you?" Mr Buchanan said, placing his finger tips together and looking at his client with a faint fresh hope.

"Till the end of the month," Atracta replied, kicking with glee again.

"The end of the month? The end of the mo
But here we are in June, and you haven't gone!"

"He never said which month," Atracta acutely
served.

Mr Buchanan gave a violent start and turned pa
Excruciating memories of Nellie Rose Fernandes stirr
in his heart and pierced it to the core. Trying to kee
his voice steady he said: "He meant April. That is wha
he meant by the end of the month. The end of April."

"But Alf came and he changed his mind. Then they
took Alf and the mistress died and he changed his mind
again. I'm destroyed," Atracta said querulously, "between
the choppin' and the changin'."

"So that he gave you notice first in April, subsequently withdrew it and gave it again after the death of
his mother. But that was in the middle of May, wasn't
it? And here we are at the end of June. What do you say
to that?"

Atracta looked bewildered and reproachful: she had
expected this man to be on her side.

"Let me put it like this," Mr Buchanan said, speaking
slowly and loudly as to a foreigner. "When are you actually leaving? When are you due to go?"

"To go?" Atracta echoed the word in horror. "I'm
not thinkin' to go. Sure, where would I go?"

Mr Buchanan closed his eyes.

Atracta decided to amplify her statement, having
now come to the conclusion that the solicitor was a per-

fect fool. "Amn't I tellin' you, I don't mind Master Michael a bit?" she said patiently. "He does be only talkin'. He couldn't contrive without me no more than a baby. There's a hundred rooms in the house and only me to tind them. And I the finest cook in the country! Dismissal, indeed! 'Tis all Master Michael's cod."

"Then how does the question of proceedings arise? What is your complaint? What," screamed Mr Buchanan, "are we talking about?"

"He did dismiss me so! And 'twas wrongful!" cried Atracta, thoroughly roused in her turn. " 'Twas a hurtful thing to say to annyone, and then to be tellin' Bridie come in me place, and she no better than a barefoot slut, and to be recountin' me deeds to the quality, and scoffin' and laughin', with talk about me all over Ireland, and Alf on all the newspapers, and Patrick with the ringworm, and the mistress would have let me keep the little chist of drawers only she died before she could say it. I, that worked me fingers to the bone for him and his, like me mother and grandmother before me! Didn't you tell me yourself, I'd get seven hundred and fifty for it? And two hundred and fifty out of that chancer Tomo? And Master Michael knows it, so he does! Wait till I tell you!" Atracta said, with a shout of laughter, "didn't he cod me, once I got into court every single blessed word I said would have to be true? Now! Tryin' to lose me the case!"

A profound silence, broken only by the ticking of the new Swiss clock, followed these words. Mr Buchanan

bowed his head, with its tightly shut eyes, over his clasped hands like a man at prayer. From the neighbouring church of Holy Souls came the sweet chime of the Angelus, and Atracta vigorously crossed herself and muttered the words. After a while Mr Buchanan raised his head and addressed his client in the passionless tones of a judge summing up.

"I have to congratulate you, madam," he said suavely, and Atracta kicked. "The finest brain at the Bar could not have demolished your case more effectively than you have done yourself. It has been a privilege to listen to you: and a lesson too, a lesson in moderation and humility. What! Only seven hundred and fifty pounds because your master, in a state of mind perhaps not too difficult to understand, tells you to go, without meaning anything by it! Only two hundred and fifty because a man drives a bull into your kitchen and gives your child a blowlamp! I now have the humiliation, the intense humiliation I may say, of telling Mulally that we withdraw; but no matter. It has been very well worth the experience."

Atracta, too entranced by the cultured voice to mark the crazed eyes and twitching hands, simpered and kicked and wriggled in her chair.

"Out! Away! Begone!" Mr Buchanan vociferated, leaping up and waving his arms like a madman. Atracta had seen something like it on the films and, still complacently simpering, went her way, wagging her hips in a manner dreadful to see. Mr Buchanan resumed his seat and buried his face in his hands, remaining in this posture for half an hour. Then he wrote a blistering letter to Mr Waverley, and went out to get drunk.

Atracta jogged homeward in the bus in a condition as near to perfect happiness as she could hope for in the absence of Mr Smith. She felt ennobled, invigorated, nourished, soothed, and appreciated. She was enjoying, indeed voluptuously giving herself up to the pleasure of, a thought better than a thousand pounds or even the chest of drawers, namely, to have occupied for over two hours the mind of a man like young Mr Buchanan. A gentleman and a great scholar like that, and he gave his whole attention to her, Atracta Smith, talked to her, was going to fight with the master for her! And how beautiful he had spoken about her at the last, calling her the finest brain at the Bar! And then, yerra, how he leaped up and shouted, the way he'd holler at the judge to give her the money! She got out of the bus at George-town gates and made her way through the grounds, wagging her hips more wildly than ever.

When she passed over the little bridge Master Michael was on the bank there, putting a fly on a rod: he was very frivolous altogether these last days, not only with the smiles and the blarney but the fishing and riding the stallion about and running off to Miss Dulcie, like there was nothing else at Georgetown to do. He looked up as her shadow fell on the water, waved his hand and blithely burst into song.

"The first day of Friday the new Pope gave to
    meeeeee . . .
A cyclamen and a little perju-reeeeee!"

he carolled.

Suddenly frightened and miserable, Atracta scuttled away into the undergrowth.

Laughing, Michael adjusted the fly and cast. The slim dark trout were moving slowly and pompously about in the brown depths of the stream and certainly would not think of rising on a fine clear evening like the present. He was fishing just for the hell of it, because there were a dozen other things he should have been doing, because he was young and happy, because he was going to sell Georgetown and marry Dulcie, very very soon now, and nobody else knew about it, not even his betrothed herself. The announcement of the intended sale should be made on his behalf by Ned Mulally, when he appeared for him in court about the rates. Sensation! He wondered who would buy it. Germans were buying up the country and being gorgeously stung too, hurrah, but he would not sell to a German. "There are limits," he remarked aloud. Better the Papists, better even the Government. Ah, for a rich philanthropic right-minded English squire, with no ambition to spend money on anything but horses and foxhounds! What a boon and a blessing he would be to their simple little community!

Busy with these delightful thoughts, relaxed and

contented on his sunny bank, he never looked up as an immensely gaunt man in black strode across the bridge and threw a long evening shadow over him. It was Father Behan, in pursuit of his parishioner Mrs Alfred Smith. In the Mater Misericordiae the day before, Father Behan had endeavoured to reach his Bishop by telephone and found himself, instead, in communication with the voluble Mr Foley: whereupon that excellent man, supernaturally informed as ever of the local doings, had gleefully reported the impending lawsuit of Moin *versus* Duff, together with his own view of the case and assessment of the damages. Sick, exhausted, in torment as Father Behan was, he had struggled from his bed this morning deaf to the entreaties of Reverend Mother and the warnings of the doctor, and made his way hither to have a word or two with the plaintiff in the case.

Returning from that duty he paused on the bridge and leaned his arms on the rail. "You never came to see me, then, Michael," he said. "And so I must come to you."

The young man raised his eyes from the water and his face brightened. "Welcome back, Father," he said, with pleasure. "And welcome to Georgetown. They told me you were sick."

"They told you I was crazy," the priest said drily. "And why wouldn't I be?"

"Divil a bit of it," Michael answered. "The sanest man in Ireland! And what brings you my way?"

"I wanted a tramp over the Georgetown lands, this

beautiful evening," Father Behan told him offhandedly. "And I thought I might run across you and maybe give you a belt, that you never came near me after the poor lady was buried."

"Ah, my hands were full with the cousin, you've no idea! And apropos," Michael said, smiling, "I want to ask you something. Did you give leave to Atracta to come to the funeral?"

"I did, of course," the priest said. "She'd never have gone to it else."

"Then why, if you don't mind my asking, why allow her but refuse my Cousin Nathaniel?" Michael persisted. The things Father Behan said and did were all somehow fascinating and important and fraught with mystery for him and this particular point had teased his mind very much.

"I do mind you asking me, so!" the priest exclaimed, in one of his quick rages. "Attend to your business, boy. Parish matters are no concern of any but his Lordship and me." The words had hardly left his lips than he became once more embroiled with the old invisible companion. "You you you!" he groaned, pressing his fists hard to his temples. "Will you never have done?"

Michael looked patiently on in silence.

"That was himself again, he has me quite driven over," said Father Behan bitterly, after a while. "Well, your cousin is not a Catholic and would hardly make one in a hundred years, and I was helping him know it. I forbade him to go to the service and he went in spite of me, as I knew he would, because to you folk blood and caste come before anything else. But I could allow Atracta, because she is Catholic to the marrow in her bones. She is," Father Behan declared, shuddering violently and with the old poignant sadness rushing back to his face, "a better Catholic than any in the parish. God help and forgive me, I sometimes think she's the only one." He drew a long quivering sigh and passed a huge hand over his eyes. "So it needn't astonish you, I'm in the Mater Misericordiae, and his Lordship himself is feeling none too well. Now God bless you, child. I will be going on."

"So soon?" Michael complained. "And you didn't give me a belt! And why don't you stay for a bit of supper? These are great days in my life."

Father Behan gave him his rare sweet smile. "Thank God for it, Michael. I was thinking your grief became you! But I'm up at Father Sweeney for the night and going to the Sisters again in the morning. You could write to me, an odd time." He strode off without another word through the dappled sun and shadow of the wood, a great tormented figure in black haranguing his familiar spirit and shaking his great clenched fists in the air: one more living testimonial, Michael thought, to the strange dark unfathomable power of Atracta Smith. And what in the name of the powers of night did he mean by calling her a better Catholic than all the others? Her, the mindless, the soulless, the unspeakable . . . Ah, but he'd better things to do than ponder Atracta who now really and truly and finally so soon would pass from his life. Smiling, he went back to his fishing. As the sun shone down and he vainly cast and cast on the clear water he crooned happily to himself like a small boy:

"The first day of Friday the new Pope gave to
    meeeee . . .
A cyclamen, a Behan, a dispinsary and a gor-
    geous perjur-eeeee . . . !"

How Ballysimon would have loved it all!

Sixteen

WHILE Mr Browning maintained a philosopher's detachment from the problems of ordinary mankind, the least little thing affecting himself would throw him into a state of painful indecision. If Dulcie were to consult him on any point concerning her own affairs he would give her his entrancing smile and say, "My poor dear child, what does it really matter?" Yet he would have the greatest difficulty in deciding even so simple a matter as whether to travel somewhere by air or by rail, returning to the mental debate time and again long after it had been, as he imagined, settled, and would keep a waiter fidgeting round him for half an hour while he chose a meal that, in any case, he would subsequently declare to be muck.

It was only when a choice was clearly present that he underwent this inner turmoil. He had resolved to marry Bridget without it because he saw no other way of keeping her always by him without paying the ridiculous sums that such people could expect in this degenerate age. His eyes had been opened by the disgraceful affair of the Buchanans' Bernadette, who had suddenly demanded a rise on the pretext that sixty pounds a year no longer went as far as in 1935, the year she began work with that family. Mrs Buchanan had reasoned patiently with her, pointing out that she was a little less active and a little more prone to sickness with every year that passed and that in fairness her pay should really be cut if anything at all; whereupon Bernadette had flounced off to a place in a Dublin hotel, leaving the Family to shift for itself.

"Disloyalty is bred in them," Mr Browning had remarked on hearing of the defection.

Having decided to freeze Bridget in her place by this bold and original method he had easily fixed on a day and an hour for apprising her of the arrangement; and with knightly courtesy intended going so far as to ring for her in the drawing room rather than in the office, where normally he would have summoned a servant with whom he had business. More troublesome than all these things together was the question of what he should wear. If he appeared in the shabby tweeds of everyday he might, by approaching the matter in so casual a way, seem to put too small a worth on himself. If he changed into the suit he kept for luncheon parties and the Ballinaduff Archaeological Society, he might be making too much of the woman, causing her perhaps to get above herself and laying the seeds of future disorder. He worked over the matter until his head ached and he could almost have cursed the subtlety of intellect that enabled him to see so many sides of a question. Finally he tossed a penny in the air, and the resulting verdict was that he was to change; and then he found that the only shirt he could wear with the suit was mislaid by the laundry and, having called down maledictions on Ireland, democracy and his two great lumps of daughters, and written a letter to the *Irish Times*, he repaired to the drawing room and rang the bell.

"Come along in, Bridget," he said pleasantly enough, although annoyance was still written large in his face. "There is something I have to say to you. You may sit down on that stool."

While Bridget perched uncomfortably on the stool, looking surprised and somewhat alarmed, Mr Browning explained to her that he was free of vulgar prejudices and a man whose actions were dictated by reason alone. Whenever he saw that such and such a course was the rational one he would pursue it without regard to public opinion. As Bridget knew he had for many years, for too many years, been deprived of the help and support of a wife; and he had now come to the conclusion in view of her high character and excellent work that she was in many ways qualified to take that place.

"It will be only right that you should have some of the privileges of a consort as well as the duties," he told her. "But I feel sure that, given our difference of station, you will respect yourself too much to look for them all. And now, Bridget, what do you say?"

Bridget had hearkened to her employer in growing stupefaction and pulled herself together with an effort. "I couldn't, sir, I really couldn't at all," she said, staring bemusedly at him.

"Then I am convinced it will work out very well," Mr Browning swept on. "Please go and call Miss Dulcie, and we will tell her our news."

"I'm after telling you, sir, I couldn't," Bridget repeated, raising her voice. "You're much too good to me altogether, but I couldn't."

Mr Browning looked at her in blank astonishment. "You couldn't?" he echoed. "Now, Bridget, what is this? How do you mean, you couldn't?"

"I'm promised to Rory McHugh these fifteen years," Bridget said shyly. "Rory wouldn't like it at all at all, he's that possessive."

There was a short, terrible silence.

"What!" the philosopher then exclaimed, in a whisper. "You! Engaged these fifteen years! You sit before me and dare . . ." He pointed with a shaking finger to the door and as Bridget went through it yelled after her, "Send Miss Dulcie here at once. At once, d'you hear?"

Left alone he moved about the drawing room in jerky little runs, tugging at his bright hair as he went. It was the sharpest hurt to the vanity he lived on that had ever befallen him and he felt almost insane. To have made an offer of marriage to a common woman and to have had it rejected! Never in the course of his ponderings on the matter had the possibility of such a turn of events even occurred to him. Atracta herself could not have writhed inwardly more than Mr Browning did as he thought of the neighbours' amusement. Thank God, the incompetence of the laundry had at least saved him from dressing up to receive this humiliation!

"I will not see that woman again, keep her from me," he chattered as Dulcie came in. He wore a face, although its expression was greatly intensified, that she knew all too well, that which appeared whenever the *Ballinaduff Mercury* failed to notice one of his cultural endeavours or he lost a game of chess. "The more you do for them, the more they expect. Trample them underfoot and they admire you. Do something for them and they despise you and give themselves airs. To think that I even asked her to sit down! I must have been mad."

Dulcie was trying not to laugh. "But, Father, if the poor woman is engaged already . . ." Convinced that Mr Browning was out of his mind, Bridget had come running to her and blurted the story out.

"Yes, for fifteen years!" Mr Browning stormed, his voice breaking on the top note.

"What of that?" In this region of long engagements, fifteen years was in the nature of whirlwind courtship.

"*What of that?* Fifteen years of treachery and duplicity? When I take a woman of that class into my service I naturally assume she will pass her working life under my roof. Yet barely five years after she entered this house she was compounding behind my back with some clod to make off and live with him in some filthy hovel up the mountain! And then, I presume, graciously to give me a couple of hours a day, if that!"

"McHugh's a decent man, and when his father dies, if he ever does, he'll be a strong farmer," Dulcie objected. "It's a good match for her. She has her own life to lead, after all."

"Don't talk such infernal nonsense," her parent scolded on, furious as a monkey. "Own life to lead! What next? But they're all the same, all the same. Your Aunt Cornelia had a Chinese cook in Singapore for eighteen years and she always said she would have trusted him with her life. Then one day she happened to go into the kitchen when the boy was out and do you know what she found?" Dulcie had heard this tale a hundred times if once. "*A drawerful of Communist literature!* Not one is to be depended on. Gratitude, loyalty, truth are words that don't exist in the native languages. And the greatest illusion one can have is to dream that there are any exceptions whatever. You're not listening," he said fiercely.

This was true: Dulcie rarely listened to her father at all. Streams of words poured into her ear and she would now and again respond with little murmurs of agreement or admiration. She knew all too well what he was going to say about anyone and anything in the world; or at least she imagined she did, for on occasion he would spring a sudden and disagreeable surprise. He did so now.

"She will have to hurry the wedding on," he said, smiling, his rage calming a little before the pleasure of what he meant to do. "She will hardly find another place with the character I shall give her."

"You know she has always been perfectly splendid," Dulcie replied. She made this remark easily and naturally, something in the way of a chicken that runs about with its head off. A moment later the terrible truth seeped in. "You cannot mean that she is to leave?" she cried in anguish.

"To leave?" Mr Browning gave a light laugh. "Do you suppose I would keep her here after what has transpired? To laugh at me behind my back? You appear singularly indifferent to the affront she has put on me."

"But, Father, you know what it is nowadays. Whom will you get in her place?"

"Really, Dulcie, that is your province, not mine. And I can see no particular need for you to get anyone," Mr Browning said, his good humour gradually returning as he watched his daughter's face. "On the whole I am well pleased with your services, and then it is high time that Anne Louise took her share in the household work. I will sell that quadruped with the foolish name so that she can give it her undivided attention." Laughing, he sat down on a sofa and picked up a worn copy of *Also sprach Zarathustra*.

Dulcie took a deep breath and tremulously said, "I'm going to be married myself quite soon."

"Nonsense, nonsense," Mr Browning murmured, lost in the Superman.

"Father, I am! Michael is to sell Georgetown and go abroad, and we are to marry first and start the new life together," Dulcie said, pressing her little hands together as if in prayer. Her engagement was blandly waved aside so often, at times she hardly believed in it herself.

Mr Browning threw Nietzsche onto a marble table and sat bolt upright. "Indeed!" he cried, shrill once more. "And what about me, pray? What about your father? Have you no thought for anyone's welfare but your own?"

"But you said you were going to marry Bridget! You were so definite, I thought you must have proposed and been accepted!"

"Kindly do not use such distasteful expressions," Mr Browning said with a fretful stamp of his foot. "Well, I am not unduly alarmed by what you tell me if it depends on young Duff selling that barn of a place up at Georgetown. Who will take it? Who can afford to keep up such places now, in these days of plebeian huggermugger? Besides, I hear he is embroiled with the law. He will find himself in Queer Street presently. And how extraordinary of him to think of marrying at this time! One way and another, he appears to have recovered from Virginia's death with enviable ease."

"That comes well from you! I still go hot and cold when I think of what you said!"

"My dear child," Mr Browning said with an air of forbearance. "You cannot conceive—how should you?— how enormously difficult it is for a man of intellect to keep it constantly focussed on the trivia of material and immediate surroundings. As well try and hold some great balloon captive with a wisp of straw. Up in the clouds? So was Socrates. Now: let us pass on to matters within your grasp. In the unlikely event of Michael Duff finding a purchaser for that white elephant of his, and if indeed you are unfilial enough to leave me when I need you most, there will be nothing for it but for Anne Louise to take full charge."

Dulcie groaned for sheer spiritual exhaustion. "Father, how can you? She is only a child. Have you any idea at all how much there is to be done here, inside and out? Even with Bridget housekeeping and cooking, I'm hard at it from six in the morning until after dark."

Mr Browning gave her his most attractive smile. "Once she gives up all that barbarous fox chivvying and futile show jumping I have no doubt but she will settle down," he replied in a reassuring manner. "Indeed, I fancy she may have to. Even in these days the despised paterfamilias is not altogether without some little say in these matters." He leaned back in his chair complacently, like a man who has solved a difficult problem amid general applause.

"It will never work," Dulcie told him bluntly. "It

is not only her youth and inexperience. Anne Louise does not like you."

If someone had fired a gun at his ear Mr Browning could not have been more shocked, amazed and horrified. "What can you mean, Dulcinea? Pray think what you are about," he exclaimed. "Not *like* me? How could Anne Louise not like me?" He stared, mouth open, over her head into an old oval looking glass with an ornate gilt frame, noting how attractively it set him off: the idea of anyone at all not liking, indeed not loving, that man, with the slim figure, the shining hair and the comely young man's face, struck him as preposterous. "Come, dear," he said kindly, "tell me you spoke in haste and let us smile over it together."

"She can hardly stay in a room with you," Dulcie replied simply. It crossed her mind that she was far from eager to do so herself, and she walked to the door. "I'm going to marry Michael and live abroad. If Bridget goes and you treat Anne Louise unfairly, we'll take her with us. And then you will be here alone." She hurried out, pulling the door so firmly after her that it was little short of a slam.

Mr Browning sat on by himself, with her last words echoing in his ears. He felt dazed, like a man who has lived through an earthquake to see the familiar contours, proportions, horizons, arrangements, thrown violently and hideously awry. He could neither recognize his surroundings nor take his bearings: all was confused, threatening and chaotic. But as the minutes passed the mental powers to which he was fond of alluding reasserted themselves and he saw the utter absurdity of his daughter's threat. Marry young Duff and take Anne Louise away, forsooth! Then who, pray, would prepare his meals, run his errands, rub his back (an ache between the shoulders being the single intimation that he was no longer exactly young), find for him pen, gloves, hat, pruning knife, string, walking stick, sealing wax, spectacles, umbrella, collar studs, all of which he lost daily once if not more, see that his morning coffee and his evening bath were really hot and just as he liked them, the former not too strong, the latter not too deep, and read the paper aloud to him after dinner in order to conserve his eyesight for things of greater importance? Surely Dulcie could not be so foolish as to suppose that Dan, or the aborigine who came in to scrub and whose name he had forgotten if he had ever known it, could assume duties and responsibilities as grave? In any event, Michael Duff would never be able to dispose of Georgetown, nor could Anne Louise leave Rougemain while she was under age. And when it came to the point, Dulcie would never forsake him: loyalty was bred in her, just as the other thing was bred in Bridget, and there was no escape. The whole ado was an example of the hysterical feminine nonsense that Nietzsche understood so well and prescribed for so soundly; and, his tranquility quite restored, Mr Browning had another lingering affectionate look at himself in the glass and, taking up *Also sprach Zarathustra* once more, soon was deep in its well-known, well-loved pages.

Michael Duff lay in his creaking four-poster bed and harkened drowsily to the rain as it drove with vehemence against the windows. His room was a vortex of draughts this July morning. He looked with love at the patch of fungus on the wall, now growing freely again and looking more like Atracta's touselled head with every day that passed. While outside the trees writhed in the wind and lashing rain, his own mind was full of thoughts that shimmered like islands in a tropical sea. It was Sunday and a hundred things waited to be done, but he lay back on the pillows and thought about Dulcie. Nowadays he thought of little else; he could afford to do so, to remember the way her hair grew, the curls at the nape of her neck under the old-fashioned knot of hair, the small hard hands, the little cream-and-honey voice, the smell of cloves that came off her skin. Until the great day when Atracta unlocked the door of his dungeon he had never dared to do it much because the misery was too great. He lay there revelling, lazily smiling, his face square, strong and gay, the image of his father in the portrait.

"Zanzibar, Zanzibar," he muttered, without knowing why.

Vaguely he grew aware of a missing note in the symphony of bedroom sounds, the rattling, creaking, sighing, flapping, that accompanied bad weather. After a while he realized that the grandfather clock had stopped. For years he had mechanically seen to it, without even noticing that he did so, and now, equally unnoticing, had let it go. He decided never to start it again. Strewn on the floor inside the case were hundreds of keys of every shape and size and age, keys tied in bunches, keys single, rusty, abandoned, that he had always intended to sort out when he got a moment. Now he would never do that. The only one of them all that he could identify was of the Georgetown strong room, a monster of a type no longer to be had and that required both hands to turn it. Michael shook with laughter, thinking how the strong room had once been burgled. Its walls were seven foot thick with a door of fitted steel, and there was a fault in the lock so that if thieves got hold of the key they still would never be able to turn it, a knack to be acquired only by long and patient effort. On the other hand there was no top to the room at all: it was roofed with a simple glass panel that smoothly opened and shut like a cucumber frame, and the burglars had climbed in and out with ease. All they found were piles of old Georgian silver, teapots, cream jugs, cutlery, kettles, trays, black with age, dumped there because no one in Georgetown would ever again have time to clean or the occasion to use them. The burglars had left at once, smashing a few windows on the way out to mark their displeasure. It was a local job, of course; someone had known of the strong room's peculiar construction but had not grasped that the Duffs were no longer as wealthy as of yore. How like them it was, the partial intelligence and the misapplied energy, Michael thought; but everything they ever did was so like them.

Now, with a harsh and grinding noise such as the millstones of God might suitably make, the door of his bedroom opened and a mop of ginger curls came slowly round it. "Master Michael, honey," a whining voice began.

"Come in, best of women, come in," said young Mr Duff in the most affable way, although the ban on her entering the room with himself inside it had never officially been lifted.

Atracta tremulously advanced a foot or two into the room and stood clawing at her apron, suspicious and apprehensive as a wild animal. "Master Michael," she faltered, "yesterda' I got Confession."

"Capital, capital. But don't tell me anything unless you really feel inclined," he said gaily, beaming at her. "I've long known where all the Guinness went to."

"And just now I'm to get Communion," Atracta proceeded, but then she broke off, overcome, while Michael listened with an air of courteous attention. Two dreadful charges Father Behan had laid upon her and she could see no sense in either one. She was to tell Michael Duff the true story of his father's death, how it was never the gunmen at all nor politics but only the hames a crowd of city boys made, how they were going to do Major Buchanan, paying him out for getting a kinsman of their own sent away, there was five of them in it and not a head between the lot, for didn't they have the directions wrong and the description wrong, God love them and help them, the creatures, and came and done Major Duff in his place, that never did harm to a soul! Everyone knew the story, only the gentry, and the Guards thought best to say nothin' for there was no bringing the poor gentleman back. The village used often have a great laugh over it. But where in the name of God was the sense of bringing it out, an old buried tale like that, and starting all the crossness again? And to Master Michael, who'd never credit a single blessed word she said about anything in the world, he was strange in that kind of way. But Father Behan insisted, and it would have to be done. Melting with terror Atracta decided now to postpone this revelation, but the other could not be postponed because Father Behan had told her she should not approach the altar until it was made.

"I was at Confession yesterda'," she began once more, in an expiring voice, and Michael smiled encouragement at her. "And Father Behan went on at me somethin' desperate the evening before, the time he came up from that city place."

Michael's smile disappeared at once as an inkling of what was to follow arose in his mind and shattered the radiant bubble there. "You saw Father Behan too? You mustn't mind him, Atracta," he said quickly and urgently, raising himself on one elbow. "You wouldn't mind him, would you? Tell me you wouldn't. Did you not say yourself that he was wrong in the head?"

"That would make no difference at all, Master Michael love, when religion came into it," Atracta revealed. "Sure, where would we all be . . ." She checked herself. "I am to beg your pardon, Master Michael, and I'm sure I do, for settin' Mr Buchanan on you, and if you were at the loss of it at all I'm to make institution from me wages. That is, if you thought of paying them an odd time, Master Michael."

"I call it a damned unwarrantable interference," Michael said angrily, sitting bolt upright and glaring at her. "Why, it is almost contempt of court! What has Father Behan to do with our affairs, and what can he know about them? How did he ever come to hear about the case at all?"

"He'll have heard them talk in the city," Atracta replied. She believed that people the world over followed Crummagh affairs with strained attention. "And Father Sweeney was after tellin' him how you were up to the house there, and Father Behan came leppin' and roarin' at me, with the old cyclamen and that, fit to be tied. So where was the sense at all in me goin' to court, if I couldn't use me discretion about what I'd say there? And anyway, Father Behan said I was not to. So now!"

It was final them, there was no hope left. If Father Behan had uttered such a decree Atracta would never in life go against it. She did not fear to offend the Almighty Himself with her lies and calumnies and frauds, but a tall crazy man in shabby black skirts and a most absurd little bonnet on his head had only to open his mouth to her and she immediately renounced them all. His lovely pretext, his honourable excuse, for cutting and running was gone, whipped from him by the only Gael he had ever liked and trusted. Even if the appeal from the new valuation should fail he still could not decently clear out now. Like many ladies of her kind and generation, Mrs Duff had possessed rather more money than she would ever admit and with the income left him he could just manage to struggle on in spite of the astronomical rating, on and on and on in the old pinched harassed back-breaking way. And that was what he would have to do. As for Dulcie . . . The tropical islands within had all vanished now, like the mirages that they had been and that, with the part of his mind inescapably geared to the frightful and the grotesque, he had always known them to be, leaving the way open to the cold stinging weather of Ireland.

"Father Behan said 'twas how you'd never let me and the young ones down," Atracta went on with a shade more confidence, for the old familiar loathing and contempt in Michael's face helped to bring her sense of security back.

He picked up a boot from the floor and hurled it with all his might.

"Get out!" he yelled. "Begone! Don't let me see you! Oh, bloody bloody bloody bloody bloody! One can't even bloody well trust you to bloody well play one false!"

With this cry of agony rent from his inmost being he lay back on the pillows again, exhausted, ruined, demented. Atracta ran happily away to her cottage to prepare herself and the triplets for Mass. There was a white lake in the haggard where Paddy had spilt one of the milk cans, the surface of it ruffled by the wind. A crowd of barnyard fowl made a rush at her, ravenous, for the men in Michael's absence were talking and smoking together in the hayloft before they walked down to church. With a part at least of the fearful disclosures made and the prospect of Mass and chapel-door gossip looming ahead, Atracta broke irresistibly into song as she went about her duties.

"Oh, the English came and tried to teach us their
    ways,
And they blamed us just for being what we are,"

she bawled, wiping Kevin's nose with a tea cloth and the farmyard mud from Patrick's shoes with his cap, before she set it on his head. She sang from a full heart as she always did sing the songs of the old country, for the concept of Ireland, the sense of being Irish, filled her with an exaltation hardly less than did that of the Faith itself.

"You might as well go try to catch a moonbea-um,"

she trumpeted on, her voice thick with emotion, as she

cleaned and pared Benedict's grimy nails with the vegetable knife,

"Or light a penny candle from a star."

"Dearly beloved brethren," Kilrany said, glowering down at them, "This is the first time I have preached
to you and I must warn you, there is no hope of its
being the last. I shall carry on for only three minutes,
less time than it takes to boil an egg or so they tell me,
but I expect you all to listen. I'm not doing this for the
hell . . . the fun of it, I promise you."

There was little need of this exhortation. Michael
Duff was comatose with despair and would not have
looked up if Kilrany had exploded a bomb. The Master
had lost a good hound over a cliff the day before and
had decided to send a bad one to heaven first thing on
the morrow and, naturally, could think of nothing else.
Dulcie was at home, cleaning the house and cooking the
luncheon, as Bridget had been driven forth; and Major
Buchanan was ill in bed, following an attempt to wash
a couple of pairs of socks. Apart from these four souls
the Protestant community to a man was drinking in
Kilrany's every word.

"I don't mind telling you, yesterday I telephoned
to old Blether . . . Canon Blessington and asked what
he was going to say," the harsh voice continued. "He
told me he was taking as text, 'The labourer is worthy
of his hire,' so I hung up. There'd hardly be a straight

face among you if I dished out stuff like that in this part of the world. Then I rang up Canon Barker and he was going to preach on 'Love your enemies.' That gave me the idea of suggesting to you this morning, dearly beloved, that with all due respect parts of the Gospel should be taken with a grain of salt. We may well *prefer* our enemies to many of our friends, and to all our relations, but if we are to *love* them, where's the point of having any? And that brings me to these Huns who are flooding the country nowadays, and to the question of Huns in general. Twice in this century our people, yours and mine, have had a crack at them. Twice we have been told that the war was over and that we must all be good friends. Did you ever hear such tommyrot? I don't care what any fool of a government may say, I know when *my* war is over and who *my* friends are. I'm still at war with Huns and always will be, and if one of them sets a toe on my land the men are ready and he'll rue the day. It is my earnest hope that some of you will follow me in this and if so, I say unto you, make your plans *now* and don't leave it until the bast . . . the fellow is actually there. I need not say that both McCarthy and I will be only too pleased to help with any technical problem you may have.

"And now I come to something which, although it is not strictly speaking religion, is every bit as important. You will have seen on the board that there is no last hymn today, the reason being that we are going to sing *God Save the Queen*, instead, God bless her. In fact we

(245)

shall do so regularly from now on, after the sermon and before I give you the blessing. It was always sung in our churches until this cockeyed grace-and-favour republic came along and while I'm running this show it always will be. We are the people we always were and we do not change our loyalties as you change a blue passport for a green. I wish you would pay attention, Michael. And you too, Master, dammit, everyone loses a hound one time or another. Well, every so often hoi polloi blows up a statue commemorating one of us. They bagged another in Dublin only the other day. Small blame and good luck to them, they are trying to obliterate their own ignoble past. But we do not have to try and obliterate our past. On the contrary, we should cling to it, head high, for we are not ashamed of it and it is all we shall ever have. And let those who despoiled us do better or half as well. Dearly beloved brethren, the time is up. To God the Father, God the Son and God the Holy Ghost, amen. And now, The Queen."

As Kilrany's little flock rose to its feet under the tattered flags, beside the Grecian urns, and lustily sang the anthem they felt that a new force and vitality had come into their spiritual life; and when the Almighty had received their last terse command concerning Her Majesty's welfare and when, heavily scowling, the shepherd had bestowed his Blessing on them, they hastened outside into the now radiant shimmering sparkling Irish summer day to go over the sermon point by point and agree it was the best in living memory.

About the Author

HONOR TRACY was born in Bury St. Edmunds, Suffolk, England. She received her education at a private boarding school in England, and later attended school in Dresden, Germany, and studied for two years at the Sorbonne in Paris.

From 1946 to 1953 Miss Tracy was a special correspondent in Europe and the Far East for the *Observer*, then Dublin correspondent to the *Sunday Times* and a foreign correspondent to the BBC's "Third Programme." At the same time she was associated with an Irish literary review edited by Seán O'Faoláin, and also contributed short stories and articles to such American publications as *Vogue, Mademoiselle* and *Harper's Bazaar*.

Honor Tracy's first book was the nonfiction work *Kakemono*, which dealt with the American occupation of Japan. Her second, a collection of essays called *Mind You, I've Said Nothing*, was published in 1953. Her reputation as one of the leading satirical humorists of the day was established once and for all with her first novel, *The Straight and Narrow Path*, published in 1956. It was resoundingly praised by the critics, many of whom called it one of the funniest books of their experience. Miss Tracy returned briefly to nonfiction with *Silk Hats and No Breakfast*, a book about Spain, and has since written four novels which are worthy successors to *The Straight and Narrow Path: The Prospects Are Pleasing* (1958); *A Number of Things* (1960); *A Season of Mists* (1961); and her latest, *The First Day of Friday*.

Miss Tracy enjoys music, gardening, walking and traveling. When she is not indulging the last-named pastime, she is at home in Achill Island, County Mayo.